Trusting TRUE NORTH

Trusting TRUE NORTH

GINA LINKO

SHADOW
MOUNTAIN
PUBLISHING

Illustrations © 2022 Kevin Keele
Interior map illustration © 2022 Rachel Murff
Compass on pages 167–170 by Drawlab19/Shutterstock.com
Text © 2022 Gina Linko

Visit us at shadowmountain.com

This is a work of fiction. Characters and events in this book are products of the author's imagination or are represented fictitiously.

Library of Congress Cataloging-in-Publication Data
CIP on file
ISBN 978-1-62972-991-6

Printed in the United States of America
Jostens, Clarksville, TN

10 9 8 7 6 5 4 3 2 1

For Clarke

Chapter 1

Dearest True,

You should investigate the phantom town of Argleton, England. You'll like the story behind it. You're a mapmaker, after all.

I visited an antique store in Manitoba before the quarantine, and I found an old map—a good one—of Minnesota. It's in French, and it calls our area *L'Étoile du Nord*, "star of the north."

The compass rose has a fancy hand-drawn fish in the middle—maybe a pike? You'll have to look at it. I've attached a photo.

I miss you, and I appreciate you taking care of little Georgie. You've been his mama while I'm gone, that's what Dad tells me. I'm proud of you, True. It's too much for Grandma Jo right now to watch him, as she's still recovering. So thank you. And you know, you might start teaching George the basics. He's old enough now.

The key. The scale. North. South. East. West.

Remember the first map you made of Spooner?
I don't think Gram would've ever gotten used to
Spooner, Minnesota, without it. It was a thing of
beauty. It still is—I kept it, you know.

I'll be home in five days. I'm counting down.

Read any good books lately? Email me back.

Love you, luv.

Mom

🌲 🌲 🌲

"Will she bring us presents again, you think, True?"
Georgie's nose was running. It was always running.

"Mom always brings us stuff. Wipe your nose." I tripped
on a half-buried glass bottle somebody had dumped near the
creek. I caught myself at the last second, then yanked the
back of George's red superhero cape before he stepped right
into the shallow, muddy water.

"Maybe she'll bring us a dog!"

"Don't get all wet. And it won't be a dog. You're obsessed."
The path—*our* path!—was nearly hidden, covered with moss
and dandelions and brambles and briars and dead leaves and
what looked like little, round pebbles of deer poop. Our path
used to be permanently worn and flattened from all our foot-
steps. Now, I had to squint in spots to make it out. A mosquito

buzzed near my ear. I swatted it away. Locusts hummed low and loud.

Is this where we usually cross the creek?

I grabbed Georgie's hand and showed him which stones to step on so our feet wouldn't get too drenched. I used to know the Scrub—or Crow Wing State Forest, if you wanted to be fancy—like the back of my hand. The strip of land that ran beside our property, beyond our chicken coop and bucking up against our vegetable garden, wasn't much of a forest, but it stretched behind us and wound north along Darling Creek for about two miles. It worked as a kind of divider for Spooner, Minnesota. Either you lived on the east side or the west side of the Scrub. That's how people around here located things.

I'd mapped the Scrub at least a dozen times, but after the lockdown, after being able to go exactly nowhere for what seemed like forever, everything seemed . . . different. Out here, away from our own backyard, everything had a fresh, new coat of *exciting* on it.

Thank the stars we're free!

Georgie said, "We should've brought flashlights. It's darker under the trees."

I rolled my eyes. *Here we go.* "We never brought flashlights last year. We're just not used to it anymore. Don't start worrying."

"You're worrying—rubbing your knuckles against your mouth."

"I am not." I jerked my hand from my lips.

3

"It means you're nervous," Georgie said. "Rosie told me so."

"Don't listen to Rose."

A frog croaked from somewhere near the muddy creek bed. George jumped at my side, scared. He was always scared, even though he wore a superhero cape most of the time. He grabbed my hand and squeezed. I squeezed it back. Each noise sounded new against my ears, and the woods itself seemed kind of weird, like a good friend you haven't seen for a whole summer.

But I was happy to be back with this friend, the Scrub.

Georgie had been driving Grandma Jo absolutely nuts with his sword-fighting this morning after e-learning. He'd used anything he could get his hands on—spatula, shoe, Swiffer sweeper. He knocked over Gram's raspberry preserves from the counter, and the glass shattered all over the kitchen floor, but she kept her cool. It was Georgie refusing to help clean up and ordering Gram to walk the plank that got to her.

She immediately threw us both out in the backyard, telling us to get out of her hair.

At the last minute, I yelped, "Can we wander around the Scrub?"

Gram had answered with a grunt.

I took it as a *yes*, even though we both knew Dad would've never agreed.

I wasn't upset with Georgie. Squeaky wheel gets the grease and all that.

"Maybe we went the wrong way. The barn didn't used to be this far." Georgie's voice sounded small.

"It's always been exactly the same amount of far," I said, studying the forest floor, the dead, wintered leaves all smothered into the ground. We had missed a lot of the spring while in lockdown. Everything was green now and growing.

I led Georgie straight ahead, watching where the sun shone through the trees. I twirled my ponytail around my finger, trying to figure out a landmark that would tell me we hadn't gotten ourselves turned around.

"Mom would have told us we should've drawn ourselves a map."

I patted his head full of curls. "Georgie, stop worrying." I tried to sound like a good older sister. Not like Rosie, all annoyed and too cool, with too many friends to worry over and her face plastered to her phone, or drawing her same horses over and over.

I took us left, which was east. I used my mini-compass necklace to check our direction, and I was right. Of course I was right. I moved a low tree branch out of our way and ducked under, holding it up for George to get under too.

"I like your other compass—the one you have at home," Georgie said.

"That one is from Mom's father, you know that."

"It has a dragon on it."

"It does."

We walked around a group of balsam and fir trees. We

followed the creek farther east. This was the right way. I recognized the overgrown railroad tracks. Then, there was the oak tree whose trunk looked like a giant had taken a bite out of it. We were definitely going the right way. The Scrub hadn't up and changed too much while we all had been quarantined.

My ribs loosened up a little, and I took a big easy breath.

"I'm hungry. I should've brought some graham crackers," Georgie said, lisping a little against his chipped front baby tooth.

"You'll live."

"I see the shiny part of the roof!" George yelped.

"Yep." There it was. Our barn. In the distance, past the bend in the creek, the trees thinned out. The barn was painted a greenish-blue. Of course, it was peeling and faded, and the whole thing slanted to the right a little like it was leaning over to get a better look at you as you came out of the trees, ready to wave hello. But it was right where we'd left it.

I dropped Georgie's hand and started to run, my ponytail swinging. The barn was where Tamsin and I had finished reading the third Percy Jackson book, where we'd drawn our Long John Silver treasure maps, where we'd buried her old cockatiel Bentley. *Rest in peace, you mean old bird.*

Back then, things were normal.

I loved this barn. Even though it wasn't technically *ours.* It was, I think, no one's. We had squatters' rights though.

"True, wait up!"

"Hurry up already!" I didn't slow.

I yanked on the sliding barn door, but it hardly budged. I had to throw all my weight into it. It was heavy, old, and half-falling apart. But I got it to move eventually. I stepped inside, and it smelled like old hay and dust and green moldy things. I liked to think maybe I smelled horses too. From a hundred years ago or so.

Shadows hovered in the far corners of the barn, but dust motes floated through the many beams of sunlight coming through the missing slats in the roof. A bird flapped its wings and flew through the largest hole in the roof. The opening was near the peak, and it revealed the lazily spinning pig weather vane that sat atop the barn.

"I think that was an owl, a great big one," Georgie whispered. And then he ran right for the rickety ladder that led up to the hayloft. The lowest rung was broken, so little Georgie had to jump up to the second one and pull himself up. He grunted but got it on the second try.

It felt good to be somewhere, anywhere, other than home.

It had been a long time since we'd . . . explored.

I remembered back at the beginning of the lockdown, when Dad said the quarantine would be good for us, would make us appreciate stuff. I didn't believe him when he said it. But right now, I was appreciating being *out of my own house and yard*.

Above me, Georgie looked over the edge of the hayloft, which was really only like a six-foot or so platform, with no rails or anything. "This is the greatest day of my life!" he called.

I wondered for a second if he was too little to be up there by himself, if it was too dangerous. I made myself picture him flailing off the edge. And landing here below.

Eh. I shrugged and decided George was a smart six-year-old.

Rosie would never take me with her anywhere, not the movies, not the bike trail out by Three Acorn Park. Nowhere. But Tamsin and I let Georgie come to the barn with us a lot. Sometimes. And he was little. Not like a totally grown-up fifth grader.

Near the far wall of the barn, I spied some equipment that I didn't remember from before. I walked over and ran my hand over the old, splintery handle of a pitchfork, bringing away a whole heap of dust. A rusty lawn mower sat behind the tools, an oil can perched on top of it. Several shovels and rakes leaned against the wall. I wondered who had been here. I mean, I knew this wasn't our property, but it had always seemed abandoned.

I realized my face was all pinched into a scowl because, after all, I liked to think of this barn as my own. Our own.

"True!" George called. "Come up here! Someone left old comic books and a whole bunch of Fruit Roll-Ups wrappers!"

"Cool," I answered him. But I was busy studying another tool that I couldn't place. It was covered in cobwebs. It had a long handle, and then something U-shaped at the end of it. There was a place to put batteries inside near the handle.

Suddenly George was over my shoulder. "Is that some kind of vacuum?"

"I wish we would've brought a flashlight after all." I lifted up the weird vacuum to look at the bottom. It reminded me of a big horseshoe.

"No, I know what that is. It's um . . . one of those . . . I love these things. Can I keep it?"

"I don't know, George. It's not ours. Anyway, what is it?"

"Oh, True, please let me keep it. It's for searching. For looking for stuff in the ground. I could have adventures! It's like, umm . . . What's it called? I saw it on YouTube when the guys were looking for treasure and the—"

A weird howling noise interrupted Georgie. We both froze in place. What was it? An animal? A person? It was a loud and low moan, and sounded like something was in pain.

It was over before it really started, but the hair on my arms still stood up. George stayed completely still next to me. I set down the weird tool, and I looked at Georgie, his eyes wide, his mouth rounded into an O.

I started to tell him, "It's nothing, I'm sure—"

But there it was again. Louder this time, like a cow mooing, but creepier, like maybe the cow was part-zombie.

"Let's go," I hissed, pulling Georgie toward the door by his elbow.

Just as we got to the door, we both turned and looked up toward the hayloft ladder. The moaning had stopped, but something was moving around. Shifting and flopping. The loose dry straw from the haybales crunched beneath the weight of . . . *something.*

There was the sound again. Low and soft, growing louder each second, the noise came from above us. A shadow crossed the large beam of light that fell through the spinning-pig section of the roof.

The moaning keyed up again, but worse even than before. It became a true howl. Then, before I knew it, it had grown into more of a scream.

George let out a yelp, and he pressed his hands to his ears. "Let's go, True!"

I pushed him ahead of me, and out we went, the sound getting worse and worse.

"Go, go, go!"

We took off running toward the Scrub, and we didn't stop until we were far, far from the barn, close to Darling Creek, the groaning zombie sounds finally covered by the whoosh of the wind, the swish of swaying branches of the trees, and the huffs of our heaving breaths from running for our lives, like a couple of real scaredy-cats.

"Was it a ghost?" George said, bending over, his hands on his knees. He had bright pink spots on his cheeks. "Had to be a ghost. I think I might've peed my pants." He grabbed his jeans. "No, false alarm. Just almost."

"Here," I said, and I pulled out his inhaler from my pocket. I didn't have a flashlight, but I always had his inhaler. I'm not a stupid kid.

George took a deep pull, and I watched carefully to see if his nostrils flared on an in-breath. They didn't. He was okay.

"You're fine," I told him.

"I know."

"I don't think it was a ghost," I said, wiping the sweat from my brow. I pulled out my cell phone. It was working. I had a signal. At the barn, sometimes I didn't. But here, it worked.

"It could've been a monster," George offered.

"It wasn't a monster."

Georgie wouldn't shut up, but we kept moving, walking now. We neared where Darling Creek was widest, probably as wide as a highway. The railroad trestle bridge sat off in the distance.

I held my phone in my hand and thought about calling Grandma Jo or Dad. But what was I going to tell them? "Help! We think we heard a ghost in the old barn, which we probably weren't supposed to be at in the first place."

No, thank you.

We had to get home. I shoved the phone into my back pocket as George sidled up against me.

"Hey." He elbowed me in the ribs. His eyes were super-wide again.

"What? We're fine, George. Calm down. Seriously, some-one was messing with us, trying to scare us from that barn, I bet—like whoever left those comic books there," I told him, halfway believing it myself. Getting angry at the thought.

But Georgie shook his head. "No, True, you gotta . . . um . . . look." He pointed, and I followed his finger.

There, under the railway trestle, far but not too far away, stood a figure, all in silhouette. It was a man's shape. Tall and stretched out, with shoulders the size of a football player. He looked about a foot taller than me, although I was pretty spindly.

He was huge. And gangly. All arms and legs, with a hood pulled up over his head like always. I knew right away who it was.

He stood there, watching us watching him. It was kind of creepy.

I narrowed my eyes at the figure. "What's *he* doing here?"

"Who is it?" Georgie asked.

"No one," I said.

The figure lifted his hand and waved, all slow-like, as if he wasn't sure at all about what he was doing.

Yep, it was him.

I didn't wave back. "Come on," I grabbed Georgie's hand and took off jogging toward the house. "That's *our* barn," I told him.

"Yes, it is," Georgie said.

"Not anyone else's."

"Are we going to tell Grandma Jo about what happened?"

George is young, but he's smart; he'd already thought it through. Just like me. We wanted to be able to go back to the barn, didn't we?

But what if it really was a ghost? Or a no-good kid trying to scare us off?

Or . . . worse?

"I don't think so," I answered Georgie. "But let me do the talking." I lifted the latch on our back fence.

"Be careful of Grandma's herbs!" George said as we closed the gate. We tiptoed through the vegetable garden.

We stood in the mudroom, taking off our sweatshirts, and I knew I wasn't going to tell Grandma Jo about what happened at the barn. It would be a mystery for George and me to solve.

It was *our* barn, after all.

"That tool—it was for metal stuff," Georgie said as we shucked our muddy boots.

"Metal stuff?"

"The tool that looked like an alien vacuum. It's a metal thingy."

"Oh, right."

"For coins."

"Yeah." I still couldn't place what the thing was. But I knew I had seen something like it before. I had the word on the tip of my tongue, but I couldn't come up with it.

George was still talking. "I could find something really special with that thing. A buried treasure. I could have a gift for Mom when she gets home, and then I would—"

"True! George! Get in here!" It was Rose's voice calling from the kitchen. I looked at George, and he looked at me. Rose wasn't usually in the kitchen. She was usually in her room, doing her high-school e-learning for twenty-four hours a day and ignoring us.

But right now, she sounded *scared*, her voice filled with trembles and shakes.

I forgot about the moaning sound in the barn really quick, and the metal tool, because when I turned the corner and found Rose standing in front of the sink, with Dad in his blue scrubs sitting at the table, and Grandma Jo giving us a real tight smile, I started to think the worst.

"What is it? What happened?" *Does someone have the virus? Someone we know?* "Is it Mom?" I squeaked.

Georgie was already hiding his face in my shirt, his arms around my waist, squeezing me for dear life.

"She's not coming home!" Rose wailed. "She's abandoned us."

Dad sighed heavy and long. "Compass Rose! You will not say that about your mother."

Mom had been gone on a job when this whole thing started, and someone on her team had tested positive. She had to stay away from us, just in case. But her quarantine was done this weekend, and she hadn't had any symptoms.

"Is she sick?" I croaked. "I talked to her yesterday, and—"

"Calm down," Dad said. "Let me talk."

Grandma Jo took ahold of my shoulders. I looked at her, and she shook her head, holding my eyes.

No, she mouthed. *Not sick.*

Dad continued, "Mom is fine. She has no symptoms. But

she *can't* come home, kids. She planned on it—she was supposed to be home this weekend—but the government closed the borders because of the virus. She can't get back until after the borders open again. Until then, your mother has to stay in Canada."

"For how long?" My words cracked, my throat suddenly too dry.

Dad shrugged and sighed. "We're not sure. It could be a while."

Georgie's shoulders shook, and his tears seeped into my T-shirt. "No, no, no," he kept repeating.

Rose cried into her hands. Grandma Jo put an arm around her and comforted her. I gritted my teeth.

We were used to Mom being gone on jobs to make her maps. But only for little bits at a time, here and there. A week at a time. Or maybe just a tiny bit longer. But this was an eternity.

It'd already been more than three weeks, and she was supposed to get home on Saturday. In three days.

Having her gone didn't used to matter that much. Not like *now.* We didn't used to count down the days until she came back, and we weren't nervous and unable to fall asleep at night. We were busy and having fun. I was going to sleepovers at Tamsin's and planning the Sister-Skate-a-Thon with Rosie. Because the world was normal and we had school and we could see our best friends and we didn't have to think about other people's germs and six-feet social distance and masks over your mouth and nose. And you didn't have to feel like everything was a whole heap scarier than it used to be. Because before, the world hadn't gone absolutely cockeyed when Mom was gone.

"She should've come home back in March," I said to Dad. I pointed my finger at him. "You thought so too. I heard you fighting about it when the shelter-in-place for Minnesota first happened. You told Mom to come right home, even though her team was quarantined," I said, my own voice quaking now. I jabbed my finger at him harder, knowing somehow, some way, some of this was his fault too. "I heard you tell her to book a flight. You two fought about it."

Dad took off his glasses and rubbed them on his scrubs, nodding along with me. "Eventually, I agreed with Mom. She wanted to be extra safe. You know that about her. She didn't realize the border . . . Neither of us did."

"We need her!" I snapped.

Georgie sobbed, "I'm scared without her!"

I held him closer as he cried. He used the edge of his cape to dab at his eyes.

Rosie chimed in, "So now we'll never get back to normal. This is all so unfair. I miss Mom." But she was already looking at her phone, her thumbs flying, talking to someone more important than us.

"Mom can't help this. Things are strange right now," Dad said. "We all have to be strong. Even if we're scared. *Especially* then."

Little Georgie's shoulders heaved. "I'm tired of being strong!" he squawked.

"George—" Dad started.

"And there's a dead ghost in the barn!" George wailed, wiping his nose on my T-shirt.

"I told you not to tell," I snapped at him.

"I'm sorry, True."

I pushed him off me, and he looked up at me with such a sorrowful little expression. I narrowed my eyes at him.

"Thanks for getting us in serious trouble," I told him.

He ran to Dad, burying his head in his shoulder, crying.

"Baby," I muttered.

"You went to the barn?" Dad asked, looking from me to Grandma Jo, who gave me a look. She raised one eyebrow at me, and I knew I was a goner.

I looked around for something to kick. "I hate this whole day," I muttered under my breath.

My throat pinched tight. I knew I was about to cry too. I knew it. And I had to get out of the kitchen before Rosie saw me and made fun of me.

"Answer me, True," Dad said.

I scowled at him. "Yes, we were at the barn. Grandma said we could go in the Scrub." I narrowed my eyes at Gram in a challenge, but she shamed me with the look she gave back.

George intervened. "We were safe, Dad. True brought masks in case anyone else was there. They weren't. Just the ghost."

"Shut it, George," I said. Why did Georgie still have to come to my rescue even after I'd been mean to him?

Dad said, "True, you know better."

"I'm tired of all these rules!" I told Dad. "Watch Georgie. Help him with his e-learning. Keep him happy. Don't go anywhere. Don't do anything at all! And now Mom's not coming home? I'm sick of it all! Doesn't she know that Georgie can't sleep at night? That he's having nightmares!"

I stalked out of the kitchen and pounded my feet up the stairs. "I'm not talking to Mom! I won't. She's left Georgie and me all on our own. We need her!"

I slammed the door to my bedroom for good measure, then flopped face-first onto my bed. I buried my face in my pillows and cried.

I cried hot, angry tears, and I pounded the mattress with my fists. None of this was fair! What did we do wrong?

Sure, *everyone* was on lockdown, but some parents were starting to let their kids see their friends outside now that it was getting warmer. They just had to wear masks. And everyone else had their moms at home, right?

Not us. Nope.

I missed her.

My mother had a British accent. She was tall and looked like an older version of Rosie. She had the most beautiful long, dark hair, all curlicues and spirals, and she smelled like the lemon dishwashing liquid she always washed up with. She called us kids "luv" all the time. She collected things with hummingbirds on them. Once in a while, she'd say "Blimey" when she was really frustrated.

I missed her so much my ribs ached when I thought about her.

I could hear Georgie, still downstairs in the kitchen with Dad, just wailing, calling for Mama.

The sound of Georgie's little voice—I couldn't take it. I pulled the pillow over my head. But the sound still shot right through me, like an arrow into the tenderest places hidden beneath my ribs.

There was nothing I could do to make it better for him.

Then, from out of nowhere, I thought of the name of the tool from the barn.

"Metal *detector*," I said out loud, my words muffled by the pillow. That's what that thing was in the barn. The tool. You skimmed it over the ground, and it would beep if there was some kind of metal beneath the soil. It was a useful tool.

For finding metal that's buried.

Like buried treasure.

I suddenly had an idea. A fantastic idea. Something to plan and do, for Georgie. To cheer him up.

To keep his mind on things that weren't the virus or Mom not coming home or the weirdo world that we were stuck in right now.

But I'd have to brave the ghost first.

Tomorrow. Right after online school.

Chapter 2

True Vincent

5th grade/Mrs. Burns block 2

Creative writing assignment

Remote e-learning day 21 (but it feels like day 323,432)

HOW-TO CARTOGRAPHY
(That's a Fancy Word for Mapmaking)

Lesson 1: Choose Your Subject

The first thing about mapmaking is this: It's about being in charge and knowing important things. You want to be smart, don't you? You do. So let's start making a map.

First, choose something you know pretty well, and that you're interested in. Like your room or your own house. If you're feeling risky, then what about your school? Or your downtown?

Get yourself some grid paper—the kind with squares on it. Big squares. One inch can equal one mile or one foot. You can choose!

You are the world's observer and recorder. But you are in charge!

First step is to walk around. Get to know your subject. Think of it like if you were a bird hovering over it, taking in each detail. Where are the landmarks placed? Like your dirty sock-pile in your room? Or your school's jungle gym? Or the mailbox where you skinned your knee in third grade? Can you see it?

Can you see it in a bird's-eye view?

I mean, I know you can't really fly, but what if you could? Can't you just imagine floating over your area? Seeing things from up there? Imagine it.

I bet you can do it.

Now, I'll help you draw it.

🌲 🌲 🌲

After school, I ignored three video-chat requests from my mother on my phone. I said a polite "No, thank you" to Gram when she tried to bribe me from my mood with my favorite cinnamon and hazelnut toast.

I ignored Rosie. She ignored me.

I sat at the partner desk I shared with Georgie, which was really two big old card tables that we had rigged up in our room, and I started mapping the Scrub. I was planning a treasure hunt for my brother.

Dad poked his head in once, asking me about my day. I answered him without even looking up.

But Georgie was a pest, at my elbow the second his

e-learning was done. "What's it a map of?" "Can I help?" "Can we go into the backyard and play pirates?" "Where's my sword?"

I finally broke down. "George, I know you want me to play with you. But right now, today, I am trying to put together something for you. Can you give me a break?"

"For *me*?"

"Yep."

"And part of it is a map?"

"Yes, now scooch. Get out of here. Quit ruining the surprise!"

"Grandma Jo! True is making me a surprise."

I sighed a very Dad-like sigh and got back to work.

Before the lockdown, when Tamsin and I read a book, we would draw the map of the place from the book as we read, revising it and taping on more and more paper to make it bigger if we needed to. When it was an old book, or a book that was set in the days of yore or something, like *Treasure Island* or *The Girl Who Drank the Moon*, we'd make our map look old too.

When we were absolutely finished with our favorite, best-looking map, we'd crumple it up, stomp on it a bit, rub a used tea bag on it, ride over it with our bike tires, and then we'd have Rose—if she wasn't too busy on her phone—light a match for us and help us burn the edges to make it look seriously antique.

I had some really good homemade maps.

The one I'd made for Georgie at the beginning of lock-down was one of my favorites. A serious pirate treasure map. George loved it so much, he taped it over the headboard of his bed. It had a skull and crossbones, like a watermark in the background, and a big fancy red X, drawn so it looked like a stamped wax seal. The ocean included several different sea monsters—some with wings—and of course, there was a super-fancy compass rose, made with true calligraphy. Tamsin had taken a class about calligraphy with her mother at the country club.

The charm of the map was in the details, Mom always said.

You decided what to include, what was important enough. What should be highlighted. What you saw when you looked at a place, whether it was real, in front of your eyes, or just in your imagination.

Your map told a story—a story from the mapmaker herself.

Mom made boring maps for the government, ones that told companies where to mine for zinc and other metals, mostly. But she collected interesting old maps.

She had one map, all yellowed and brittle from being seriously old, framed in our hallway. It was older than Gram. It showed Kew Gardens in London, where Mom was from. She drew her first maps there, she always told us. Fell in love with hummingbirds there.

But in a trunk in the basement, Mom had a whole mess of maps—antique ones with curlicue handwriting that was really hard to read, ones with fancy angels drawn in the corners who were blowing winds to take the sailors home, ones with mermaids off the coasts, and the old saying, "Here be dragons!" written in the area of the map that was still unexplored. Unknown.

It's a whole saying that early mapmakers made famous. It's what they wrote when they didn't yet know what was there. *HC SVNT DRACONES*. It was Latin.

Here be dragons.

Could there be a dragon in that hayloft? Maybe. One that moaned and groaned and scared me away. For now.

But I could slay that dragon, and I could "borrow" that metal detector for Georgie to go looking for buried treasure with the map I was making him.

I was going to face that ghost or dragon or whatever it was. It felt good to have something I could slay.

But of course, I had to get creative. Because I totally wasn't allowed to go back to that barn, because, well . . . Life. Rules. Grandma Jo. Dad.

And everyone was giving me the skunk eye today, as if they knew I was going to try to sneak out.

But little did they know, I could do anything *under the cover of dark*—I loved that saying. I'd read it in the Sarina Clutter mysteries that Tamsin and I had both been reading over lockdown. I texted the saying to Tamsin while I was working on my map, telling her I was going on a quest *under the cover of dark*, and she had to come with me on video chat.

Because I could do it alone. I *would.*

But I wasn't about to pretend I wasn't scared about it.

While I worked on my map, I also worked on my braveness. I thought about how happy Georgie would be with my new buried treasure plan.

Georgie had fallen asleep pretty quick, and I quietly squirmed out of our room at eight p.m., armed with only a flashlight and my phone, which was pretty old and junky and not brand-new like Tamsin's but still worked okay if you only ran one app at a time.

I hoped he wouldn't wake up until I was back from the barn.

I told myself it was probably just a wounded animal. Not a ghost. More like a hurt baby racoon. Or an owl nest full of babies that were moaning as they hatched from zombie eggs. A bunch of grizzly looking owls bumbling around and searching for some brains to eat, moaning the word, "Whooo!"

Ugh. I couldn't let my imagination get the best of me. I couldn't. I thought instead of how Mom would react if told her about the groaning business at the barn. "Pishposh," she would say, waving her hand, and that would be that. She didn't have time for such silliness.

My phone buzzed when I got into the mudroom. Tamsin was calling me. I'd already caught her up over text on what had happened at the barn earlier and what my plan was for tonight.

I answered, barely a whisper. "Hold on a sec."

"I can't believe you're doing this. You're seriously brave."

"Tamsin, shh. You have to wait until I get out of the house."

I shoved my feet into my boots. I tried to close the mudroom door quietly, but there was always a closing squeak. I stood totally still on the outside steps, and I waited, half-expecting to hear Dad's voice. But then I reminded myself he was at work. The night shift at the ER.

I didn't hear anyone knocking around in the house. Gram was probably watching her late-night TV cooking shows. I hauled across the backyard, past Mom's hummingbird feeders, past the chicken coop.

"True?" Tamsin persisted.

"Okay, okay, I'm on my way. I'm opening the latch of the back fence now."

"Aw, I miss your chickens. How's the Colonel?" Tamsin asked, referring to our rooster.

"Still waking us up at the crack of dawn. Still crabby as always."

I hurried into the Scrub, nearly tripping over the old tire that sat on the forest floor, right at the path's opening. I'd stepped around that thing for years, but everything back here looked creepier in the shadows. Much creepier. Everything was worse than I thought it would be. Even Gram's wind chime hanging off the porch gave off a sinister little tinkling sound. Every shadow was creepy. Every tree branch too.

The pine cones crunching under my foot: creepy.

The frogs croaking: creepy.

The wind rustling the leaves: creepy.

The bugs buzzing around my ears: even creepier.

"But what if you get there, and it *is actually* a ghost?" Tamsin asked.

"I don't think I believe in ghosts. Or if I do, maybe they could be good ghosts, just wanting to hang out and get a chance to play their favorite video game again."

"I wish I could be there with you."

"I know."

"I miss you, True. All I do by myself is boring stuff, but if I could be with you we'd be doing the same boring stuff, but together. We could make those lemonade ice pops with sprinkles, and we could try different lip glosses, like the ones that come in the pack of, like, twelve. All the flavors you could imagine—like chocolate pudding lip gloss. *Ew*. And we could prank call Miles McAlvoy!"

Yuck. Sometimes lately Tamsin didn't sound like she knew what I liked anymore. "Or we could start the next Percy Jackson together," I offered.

"Exactly. That too. My mother totally says we can see each other—just outside, you know. Why won't your dad let us?"

A twig snapped beneath my shoe, and the broken bits caught on something. I tripped and toppled forward, falling to my knees. I dropped my phone and the flashlight. My hands landed in some mud.

"Oh figs," I said, using Grandma Jo's faux swear word.

I picked up the flashlight but couldn't find my phone. It must've landed face down. I heard Tamsin's voice. "True? True? You okay? Should I call 911?"

I spotted my phone and grabbed it. "Don't call 911! I just dropped my phone for a sec."

"Well, darn it, True, you're going to have to answer me then. Don't drop the phone, because, I will tell you what, I've always admired your bravery, True Vincent, but this set of shenanigans is about to put me over the edge. I'm, like, dialing 911 the second you don't respond. Got it?"

"Settle down, Tamsin. You know the phone always cuts off reception near the barn." Just saying the words sent a shiver down the back of my neck.

"Maybe you should turn back."

I neared the railroad trestle. My nerves were certainly starting to act up, making my palms all sweaty and my skin feeling too jumpy on my bones. But I told Tamsin, "I'm too close. I can't turn back."

"True."

"Just keep talking to me, Tams, then I won't feel alone."

"Umm . . . suddenly, I can't remember a thing to say. Umm . . . "

"Seriously?"

Something flapped its wings, and I nearly dropped the phone again. "Ah!"

"What was that?"

"I don't know. Maybe an owl or a bat. Or a pterodactyl."

Tamsin giggled.

I hurried my steps, and I pointed the flashlight toward the trestle. "I saw Kyler Grier out here last time."

"Kyler? The big scary kid?"

"Yeah."

"Out here, where?"

"Not the barn, but beneath the railroad tracks. He was looking at Georgie and me when we were running away from the barn."

"He's so weird. You know, Miles and Dakota don't like him. After the whole thing . . . "

"Well, on the bus, before the lockdown, Oliver Kennedy said that Kyler is actually really nice, that Fitz and those guys bullied him into that fight." Mom always told me to make up my own mind about people, and Kyler had never done anything to me.

Tamsin continued, "He kind of creeps me out though. He's so huge. Looks like he could eat me for breakfast."

"Yeah, his fist must be the size of a meat loaf."

I neared the big set of pine trees and rounded the east side of them. The path looked more worn down this time. Already.

"Mmm," said Tamsin, "I miss Grandma Jo's meat loaf."

"Grandma Jo misses you too."

I neared the edge of the Scrub. The moon had lit up the night so clearly. Not a cloud in the sky. I stopped, looking at how the moonlight glinted off the metal patchwork on the west side of the barn roof. I smiled at seeing the familiar slant of the building.

Hello, barn.

"It'll probably be so dark inside there now," I said.

Tamsin's voice was a whisper. "True, what if it *is* a ghost?"

"Nope. It has to be an animal."

"It could be like a really gross ghost, like blood and guts and brains."

"That sounds more like a zombie."

Tamsin paused, then said quietly, "I'm sorry your mom isn't coming back soon."

"Thanks, Tams. But that's why I have to do this. I need to get that metal detector for Georgie. It'll give him something to be excited about."

"I know."

"'Cause this whole thing with Mom makes him sad. He needs someone."

"He does," said Tams. "I hate thinking of Georgie being sad."

I'm sad too, I thought to myself. It was true. My anger was starting to fade into a sort of helpless, sad feeling, which was kind of worse. It made me scared.

"What if it's, like, a homeless person inside the barn?" I said, changing the subject, turning the phone so Tamsin could see how spooky the barn looked in the moonlight.

"Somebody could be hiding in the barn. Like someone who did something bad—really bad—and is hiding from the cops."

"Maybe they robbed a bank? Or lit a school on fire? And before they were, like, trying to scare you away with all that ghost business?"

"I really want to get that metal detector for Georgie though. It'll give him the coolest treasure hunt."

"The best treasure hunt."

"Yeah."

"You going to draw a map?"

"Already started." I took a few more steps toward the barn and was almost there, when I realized the door was closed.

Georgie and I hadn't had time to close the door before we left yesterday afternoon.

No way.

Someone else had been here between then and now.

Was maybe still here.

"Tamsin, I think—" But when I looked at the phone, I saw the connection had been broken. I knew reception was bad near the barn. But it still surprised me. Spooked me.

I pocketed my phone. My knees knocked, and my palms sweated. I swallowed hard against the nerves in my throat, and I grabbed the handle of the barn door before I could let myself chicken out.

I was here, taking care of Georgie. This was *our* barn.

And I needed that metal detector.

I could be in and out in two seconds. Ten tops.

I didn't need to investigate the moans and groans. Nope. Just in and out.

Sliding the barn door open, I stepped inside. My eyes adjusted to the darkness, but the moonlight helped a lot. My ears searched the sounds of the night, and I heard crickets and the bullfrogs from the creek, but so far . . . no zombies.

The lawn mower and tools still stood in the corner. The whole place looked pretty much the same as it had yesterday afternoon, only now everything was cast in a purple, moonlit glow. I held my breath and steered clear of the hayloft ladder. No reason to get any closer to the moaning, bellowing *creature* if I didn't have to.

I skimmed along the western wall of the barn, toward the metal detector.

I had just grabbed the handle, when, out of the corner of my eye, I caught something move, like a shadow. A blip of movement. I froze. I turned my head a fraction to see.

Some *thing* was coming down the hayloft ladder.

Something shadowed and dark, looming and large.

It missed the last, broken rung of the ladder and landed with a thud on the ground. "Ow! Gotta fix that."

I rubbed my knuckles against my lips. Could ghosts hurt themselves falling off ladders? What about zombies? I pictured bloody gashes and trailing guts and oozing brains.

I wanted to scream.

I hated this stupid plan. I wanted to go home.

I wanted Mom.

I wanted Rosie and Dad. I wanted Grandma Jo to yell at me.

The dark figure stood up. It turned toward the door, and then looked back up toward the hayloft. The figure had something cradled in his arm. A bag of stolen money? A severed head?

But no, the moonlight hit the figure just right, and I saw it was stupid Kyler Grier, carrying a bunch of . . . towels?

His black hoodie was pulled up around his face. His shoulders were wide as a coat hanger. He mumbled something to himself, looked up again at the hayloft, and shook his head. Then he turned and left, closing the big barn door behind him.

I waited for a few long seconds, then finally breathed again.

He hadn't seen me. And he hadn't noticed I'd opened the barn door.

I stood for a long time in my dark little corner of the barn, holding on to the metal detector, unsure what I was going to do, what Kyler was doing here. Was he hiding here? Hanging out here?

Had he scared me away with the moaning yesterday?

Why?

But, no, it couldn't have been him, because he was all the way at the trestle when Georgie and I were running away.

So what had made those noises? And what was Kyler doing here now?

I was shaking off the whole weird scenario, trying to sneak out the barn door, peeking to make sure Kyler had gone far away, when I heard a tiny, barely there mewling voice coming from up in the hayloft.

It was a pathetic little noise. Not scary at all.

Just a breath and a scratch-scratch of a voice.

I considered leaving with the metal detector and hauling home.

But I couldn't. Something in me wanted to know what was going on. I clicked on my flashlight. I shone the beam up to the top of the ladder.

There—a shadow. Something small. It scurried away.

I argued with myself for a good twenty seconds or so. But of course I had to look. I had to go see.

I squared my shoulders and thought of Mom. *Pishposh!*

I set the metal detector down, put the flashlight between my teeth, and climbed up the hayloft ladder. There, under the west eaves, right smack in a funnel of moonlight, was a nest made out of an old quilt and what looked like a ratty, old Spooner Middle School gym uniform in faded blue and gold. Sitting in a heap—a sleepy, squirmy little heap—were three or four tiny kittens. A pile of whiskers and fur and tiny pink noses.

"Hello, there," I whispered. I knelt down to get a better look.

The orange one blinked open his eyes at me and mewled a hello. He stood on shaky little legs and stretched. At first glance, I thought there was only one huge black-and-white kitten in the heap, but upon further inspection, I realized they were two different tuxedo kittens—one had a black mark that looked like a mustache right under his nose, and the other had a spot in the shape of an arrowhead over his eye. The two kittens had been curled really tight against each other.

The orange one continued to meow at me, stretching more and walking over to investigate. He was the spokesperson, the one I assumed had made the racket at me from the top of the ladder.

He continued meowing and pleading his case. I felt like he was telling me about the fourth kitten. Because there was his brother, the tiniest of the litter, all black, sleek as oil. The orange kitten nosed him.

The black one's eyes were not even open, his eyelids seemed so very tender and thin.

"Oh, bub, it's okay," I told the orange cat, and I tried petting him. He seemed okay with it, bumping his head into my hand, purring like a motorboat. "What's wrong with your brother?"

I gently touched the black cat, and, at first, he didn't move, but quickly, I felt the slightest squirm. He was alive. I let out a worried breath.

Suddenly, from behind me came a hiss. A loud and frenzied noise. I turned, and there was Mama Cat, a large orange tabby with her fur all standing up and her back arched like a Halloween cat.

She hissed again. And hopped toward me.

I fell onto my butt and scooted backward, my hands feeling for the edge of the hayloft. I didn't want to fall off, but I also didn't want to get scratched to death by this mama cat either.

I was far enough away that Mama backed off a little. I slowly stood up and backed away as she rounded toward me, getting in between me and her kittens.

She was a good mama. Always there when her itty-bitties needed her. She thought maybe I was going to hurt them. I understood.

"I'm leaving," I told her. "I wouldn't hurt them."

And then the mama cat sniffed the heap of kittens, spending a lot of time on the little black runt, licking his face, his nose, his closed eyes.

Is he okay?

She settled around her babies, but I could tell something was wrong by the way she moved. Something was hurting the mama. She moved gingerly, limping some.

I crouched down again to get a better look at all of them. "You okay, Mama Cat?" I asked.

She growled a low warning. I'd gotten too close again.

And there was something in that growl that reminded me of the ghost.

"Was it you the whole time? Were you moaning when you were having these here babies?"

Then, through the slats of the barn, the beam of a

flashlight shone through, jostling and bouncing its way toward the barn.

"Oh no, someone's coming."

I heard the crunch of shoes on gravel. I looked around. I couldn't get caught in here. What if it was Kyler again? But what if I sneaked out and he was coming back here to hurt these kittens? Or steal them from their mama?

My mind flew in a million directions.

I hurried down the hayloft ladder, skipping the last rung, landing on the floor of the barn on my butt, just as the barn door started to open.

I lurched for the dark corner near the tools. I crouched low near the lawn mower, and my pulse pounded loud in my ears. I couldn't hear exactly what he called up to the hayloft because my own heartbeat was too loud, but I could tell it was Kyler Grier.

And then he was climbing up the hayloft ladder, making kissing noises toward the kittens.

Kyler?

The same kid who had knocked out one of the Sullivan twin's back teeth? It was a baby tooth, but still.

I didn't stick around to see what else he was doing, though. I grabbed the metal detector. I felt a little, tiny flash of guilt for "borrowing" it, but I would return it. Right quick. Before anyone missed it.

Rules. I had just about had it with them lately.

I slowly skulked my way along the edge of the barn

toward the open door. If Kyler saw me, he didn't say a word. He seemed too busy talking to the kittens in a baby voice, one that was so cute and tender it made me smile.

I thought I heard him use the word "smoochies."

Even so, I hauled out of there, not stopping until I was deep into the Scrub.

A train whistled in the distance, and I pulled out my phone, dialed Tamsin.

"You're okay? You're alive?" she squawked.

"I'm fine," I said. "Just out of breath. You'll never guess—"

"It was a ghost after all!"

"Kittens."

"Kittens?"

"Yeah, and I got the metal detector!" I laughed then, too loudly. The sound echoed against the quiet trees in the forest, overpowering the soft music of crickets and rustling leaves. But then the whistling train neared the trestle bridge, and the click-clack of the tracks filled up the silence of the Scrub.

I reminded myself I was outside in the middle of the night, where I wasn't supposed to be, all by myself. I hurried back on the path toward home.

"How many kittens?" Tamsin asked.

"Four."

"I wish I could go back there with you."

"I do too. I think I'll have to take Georgie to see them."

"You have to text me pictures."

I spoke to Tamsin the whole way back home. I told her

about the two black-and-white ones, the little orange tabby, the mom with the limp, and the little black one that I was really worried about.

I didn't, however, tell Tamsin about Kyler Grier.

I wasn't exactly sure why, but I was keeping a secret inside a secret.

Chapter 3

True Vincent

5th grade/Mrs. Burns block 2

Creative writing assignment

Remote e-learning day 26

Lesson 2: Scales for Kicks

Mapmaking for Kids

My mom always says that you could measure every distance in and around Stonehenge with a Hershey's bar, but why would you? I don't know, but it sounds pretty fun to me!

Every map has a scale. It shows you the distance from one point to another. Usually, it's something like one inch equals one mile. But you're going to make your own scale.

First, find something to measure with. Maybe something that is a standard size. Like a deck of cards or a Jenga block. Pro tip: I think it's more fun to use something that is not a standard size. Like, a younger brother. A shoelace. A backpack. Or—just for funsies—a spatula. Whatever you want.*

Second, choose a straight sort of place to measure. How about from your front door to the sidewalk?

Now, using your spatula or whatever you chose, measure it out. Start by the front door, lay down the spatula, and then use your finger to hold the spot where it ends. Then lift up the spatula, move it to the new start point, and put it down again. Repeat until you're at the sidewalk.

So there you go. The distance from the front door to the sidewalk is how many spatulas?

Once you have that number, you can draw that on your map. So each square on your grid-paper could equal one spatula, or whatever you used to measure. See what I mean? You can measure pretty much anything with anything.

But when someone else goes to follow your map, they might have a spatula that is a different length than yours—and that's where the problems start. That's why we use standard units of measurement like inches or feet or miles! That way anyone can follow your map no matter how long their spatula is.

*One time I measured the width of my backyard using an éclair—even though my mother told me over and over not to—but then my brother took a big sloppy bite out of the eclair before I was finished, so I would not recommend this tactic.

🌲 🌲 🌲

"You can follow the map," Grandma Jo said to Georgie, "but you're always with your sister. And if you see anyone, you stay away. We're careful, right? Six feet, got it?"

"Got it. The virus. Six feet," Georgie answered. He used his robot voice, the one he always used when talking to Gram, so it would match hers.

Right before she came to live with us a few months ago, Gram had her voice box removed because of cancer. So now she could only talk if she put this fancy device up against her throat—to act as her new techno voice box—and even then, she still sounded a bit like a robot.

But she liked when Georgie imitated her. It always made her smile.

Same way Georgie imitated Mom's British accent. He liked to say he needed to go "to the loo." He also called her "Mum" sometimes and referred to Dad as "luv."

No. I wasn't going to think about Mom.

"Gram," Rose said from the top of the stairs. "Do I have to clean the chicken coop?"

"Yes, Rosie," she answered. "You know it's your job."

Rose answered with a sigh. One time, I remembered Grandma Jo saying that Rose had inherited Dad's language of sighs. I smiled thinking of that.

Rose had more chores to do lately. We all did. Dad's unit at the hospital had turned into a virus unit yesterday. So when Dad was home, he stayed away from us, in the basement, where we had a foldout couch, an old TV, and a lonely old toilet sitting out in the open. But it worked.

Dad was kinda sorta quarantined, but not really. He still came up to the kitchen. I saw him this morning, but he was wearing a mask, one with Paw Patrol characters on it. Dad's usual job was as a nurse in the children's unit. But now, I guess all the people available had to work to help people with the virus.

"How you doing, True?" Dad asked me that morning.

I'd been finalizing my map for Georgie. I had the big paper out—the butcher paper, as Mom called it—rolled out over the kitchen table, and I was using Mom's good colored pencils. I was waiting for Dad to tell me not to. But he didn't.

"I'm good," I answered.

"That's looking professional," he said, motioning to the paper. "I like the details."

I nodded. I didn't want him asking too many questions because if he knew what I was really doing, leading Georgie on a treasure hunt, he might put some limits on where we could and could not go, and you know that old saying—*what he doesn't know won't hurt him.*

Dad sat at the table across from me and traced his finger over the compass rose I'd drawn out of arrows and swords, a Jolly Roger flag floating high in the background. "Your mom said you wouldn't answer her calls last night."

"Nope." I worked on the railroad trestle bridge, erasing and starting over again, trying to get the shape of it right.

Instead of a standard scale to the map, like inches equaling miles, I chose one square equals six GPs—or Georgie Paces. That was one rule of mapmaking I loved. You were the boss. You could make it however you wanted.

"You can't give your mother the silent treatment forever," Dad said.

Or can I?

I almost said it out loud, but I didn't. I busied myself with my map.

Dad gave his biggest sigh to date, a large, disappointed whoosh of air inside his Paw Patrol mask. But then he got up, put the lid on his favorite silver to-go coffee cup, and gathered up the rest of his stuff for work.

"Have a good day," I'd told him.

Mom liked to say Dad was the strong, silent type. I appreciated in a weird way that he'd tried to talk to me, even if I didn't want to talk.

He was gone now, away at work, and the map was officially finished. Plus, Grandma Jo was an easier mark. She liked to say that she let us have *more leash.* "You kids need to roam," she often said. Or at least she used to. Before the lockdown. Remembering that kind of pinched something tight underneath my ribs. I missed our freedom.

"Georgie, you're going to need your backpack," I told him.

"Yes, Captain!"

"And bring a water bottle. We might be gone a while."

"Not past lunch," Gram said. "And *no barn.*"

"Okay," I said.

Of course, I told myself it didn't really count. I had my fingers crossed behind my back. Besides, I *maybe* wasn't going back there. *Maybe.*

Georgie came back in the kitchen with his backpack on—and an eyepatch. "Aye, aye, Captain."

"Really?"

"You said it was a treasure hunt."

"It is."

"Onward!" He lifted an old cardboard wrapping-paper tube like it was a sword, pointing it toward the back door, smiling big, his dimples showing.

I smiled too. You had to love Georgie.

"Grab your inhaler," Gram told him.

And we were off.

♠ ♣ ♠

"You swashbuckling matey!" George said to no one in particular as we wound through the path in the woods. He was using his cardboard-tube sword as a crutch for a pretend wooden leg. At least, I think that was what he was doing.

George squinted at the map. "How many Georgie Paces am I supposed to take along this path?"

"You might have to measure on the map itself. Take out your ruler."

"I can eyeball it. With my one eyeball."

I'd gotten up super early. I'd put new batteries in the metal detector, and sure enough, it worked. I'd run out into the forest with it, along with two golden dollar coins I'd gotten from the tooth fairy about a hundred years ago. I stashed the metal detector behind a tree and buried the coins out by the railroad trestle. I told myself it was because it would be easy to lead Georgie to that spot, easy for him to recognize the landmark of the trestle on the map.

But . . .

I was still thinking about those kittens, their poor mama. Of course I was.

I wanted to go to the barn.

"So, um, I got you a little something to help on your hunt," I told Georgie. I walked over to the oak tree with the trunk in the shape of a Y near the creek and pulled out the metal detector for him to see. Georgie's mouth fell open.

"Blimey, Captain!"

"You know how this thing works, right?"

"Can I turn it on?" He dropped his cardboard-tube sword on the ground and grabbed the metal detector from my hand. "I can turn it on . . . " He used both hands to carefully hold it, letting the handle balance on his little shoulder. The thing was taller than he was. He flicked the switch.

He moved it along the ground, dragging it really. The machine let out a series of plain, even beeps.

"You have to kind of let it hover, not hit the ground."

"Okay," he said, biting his lower lip like he did when he was concentrating.

Beep . . . beep . . . beep.

"Can you hold the map? And I'll, like, walk with this?" he asked.

"Aye, aye, matey," I told him, happy to see him so charged up about this.

I picked up his cardboard-tube sword, and I took the map from him, holding it out for both of us to look at. "Where do we need to go?"

"I think . . . looks like about twenty Georgie Paces to the old pile of bricks on the other side of the creek."

"Okay."

But then Georgie pointed the other way, away from the trestle bridge.

"Nope, wrong way," I said. "You're not thinking of this right."

"What do you mean?"

"You're thinking of it upside down. Which way is always at the top of the map?"

"North. True North, like your name. True North Vincent."

"Right. So north is the top of the map. But which way is north here, where we are standing in the Scrub?"

"Oh. I don't know." He bit his lip, then pointed south.

"That's why you're turned around. It's this way," I corrected him.

"Got it!" He was off and running, as best as he could, balancing the metal detector on his shoulder.

Beep . . . beep . . . beep.

I caught up to him. "You know, they used to not always put north at the top. Sometimes it was east. That's where they came up with the term *orient*. They had to *orient* the map—turn it the right way."

But Georgie wasn't listening. He was really moving, taking his Georgie Paces seriously, counting them out loud.

Suddenly, the metal detector beat a faster rhythm. *Beepbeepbeep!*

George turned to me, his mouth in an O. "I want to dig!" he called out.

"I guess we better dig!" I said. We weren't at the trestle yet, but who knew?

"The shovel, Captain?"

"Aye, aye." The "shovel" was nothing more than a garden digger, but I knew Georgie needed it to be a shovel from pirate times, so I agreed. I got it out of my backpack.

We both got on our hands and knees, and in no time flat, Georgie had uncovered two old nails, one straight and one twisty, both rusty and pretty crusty. He seemed both proud and slightly disappointed. "Batten down the hatches!" he called out. He stood up, pocketing the nails. "We have a treasure to find!"

We ran to the trestle bridge pretty quickly, and it was clear where I had dug earlier. If Georgie had been paying closer attention he would've seen it, no problem. But he was studying the map, not the earth, and that was okay too.

"The X marks the spot, Captain. And the X is on this side of the trestle bridge," he said. I puffed up with pride, because Georgie was reading the map correctly.

Mom would be so proud. I was teaching him how to read a map. Soon, he would probably make his own, and Mom—

No.

I wasn't going to think about Mom.

George walked slowly around the spot near the trestle's edge, and he passed the metal detector over the area, the steady beep unchanging.

But then he hit the right spot, and the beeping went crazy.

Beepbeepbeepbeep!

"True! I found it!"

He dropped to his knees, and this time, he forgot all about his shovel. He dug with his hands in the loose dirt. "What is it, True? What do you think it is?"

I almost said, "I buried it here, dummy," but I knew enough to bite my tongue.

Quickly, he had the two golden dollars in his hand, and he was smiling up at me, his face smeared with dirt. "Treasure!" He kissed the coins and then pocketed them. "Is there more?"

"Maybe . . ." I looked past the trestle bridge, in the direction of the blue barn. "But it's not exactly on the map."

"What are you thinking, True?"

"We could take a look over at the barn, see if we turn up anything metal."

"Did you forget about the ghost, Captain?"

"Well, I didn't exactly tell you, but I did some exploring on my own, and I figured out what the ghost was, and—"

"True! Dad is gonna be so mad at—"

I put my hands on my hips and glared at George. "He's not going to find out, is he? And neither is Grandma Jo! Right?" I challenged.

George shook his head. "So what was the ghost?"

"It was a lot less scary than you might think."

"Really?"

"Really."

"But you have to promise to keep it a secret." I felt a squeeze of guilt asking Georgie to keep this a secret. I ignored it best I could. "I'll buy you ten boxes of graham crackers."

Georgie squinted at me, considering. "Yep. I can keep it a secret." Graham crackers were his kryptonite.

"No, but seriously. You have to actually keep it. Not like last time."

Georgie spit in the dirt, used his heel to push dirt over it, and raised up two fingers in some kind of salute I was pretty sure he just made up on the spot. "Pirate's honor!"

I rolled my eyes. "Alright, follow me, kid."

🌲 🌲 🌲

"Where are you taking me, Captain?" Georgie climbed up the hayloft ladder behind me. Of course, he insisted on bringing the darn metal detector, so every step up was a jumble of *jingle-jangle clink-clank* noises.

"Georgie, stop with the pirate stuff, okay? And you're going want to have both eyes for what I'm about to show you. Lose the eyepatch."

When we got up to the hayloft, I looked around. In the daylight, I noticed there was a stack of comic books in the corner near the cats, an empty Gatorade bottle, and an old lawn chair folded and leaning against the wall. Someone was hanging out up here.

I think I knew who.

"You are kidding me! Kittens?" Georgie yelped, dropping to his knees and staring at the four little sausages. They looked bigger already, all sleeping in their little cuddle. The three bigger kittens were nestled on top of the old patchwork quilt, while the runt sat off to the side on the blue-and-gold gym shorts. He seemed scrawnier than before; even his eyes were still closed.

"Can I pet them?" George asked.

The orange tabby kitten had woken and was up and meowing, rubbing his head on Georgie's knees.

"I think so."

George scratched the top of the leader's head. The kitten answered with a purr. "They're all boys," George announced.

"How do you know that?"

George shrugged at me. "I don't. I just *think*."

I rolled my eyes.

I looked around for the mother, but she was nowhere to be found. I hoped she was okay. I remembered her limp, her crabbiness. "The mum is probably out hunting for mice or something."

"The 'mum'?" Georgie said. "You sound like Mom."

"Yeah," I answered quietly. I was missing our mom something fierce in that moment.

"There's four, right? Those two black-and-white ones are twins." They too were up, nudging their heads against Georgie's legs and mewling at him. They all wanted his pets and attention. "That one is Mustache. This one is Eyepatch. And you, my loud friend, are named Mr. Orange."

George was sitting cross-legged, pretty much covered in kittens. He looked over at the runt, who still hadn't stirred. "Is that one okay?"

"I don't know," I said, but I settled on my knees right beside it. I petted the top of its head, and it squirmed into my touch a little bit, but barely moved. I touched the bottoms of its tiny paw-pads, pressing them gently to see its claws. Its whiskers twitched.

"He seems like an Alfred," Georgie said.

"No, her name is Teacup."

"You already named him?"

"Yeah, and it's a her," I told him, although, of course, I didn't know.

"Oh, come on, True! They're all brothers."

"No way. She's a girl. I say so."

Georgie huffed.

A voice boomed, "What did you say you named her?"

Georgie and I gasped, both turning around to see Kyler Grier's head peeping up over the ledge of the hayloft.

Chapter 4

"Who are you?" Georgie said. He attempted to lunge for his cardboard-tube sword, while still covered in kittens.

"George," I said. I shook my head at him. "This is Kyler. I know him."

Kyler climbed up the rest of the way into the hayloft, his tall body taking up a lot of space. He had to duck his head when he stood up. He moved far away from us, not toward the kittens. Then he answered Georgie, "I was in your sister's class. Before the lockdown."

"You're in fifth grade? You're ginormous!"

"George, be nice."

"That *is* being nice. It's a fact. He's ginormous. I wish I was ginormous. Another fact. I'm George Vincent. George Bacon Vincent. I'm named after a famous London carf-tographer. Are those your comic books?"

George had gotten to his feet while he talked. He held Mr. Orange in the crook of his arm, petting the cat as it purred loudly. George walked a few steps closer to Kyler.

"Stay here, George." I yanked on his hoodie.

Kyler's face fell. "I'm not gonna hurt him."

"I just meant 'cause of the virus. Six feet and all that."

"Yeah, you're right. I forgot," Kyler said. "I'm not used to seeing people." He reached into his pocket and put on a blue mask, one that looked a lot like the paper masks my dad sometimes wore at work.

"Have you been taking care of these kittens?" I gestured to the old gym uniform, the quilt.

Kyler shrugged. "I haven't really taken care of them exactly. Just keeping them company, I guess you could say. They like it when I read to them."

I studied his face, what I could see of it above the mask. I didn't know if he was kidding or not. "The other night, I was here—"

"Yeah, I saw you leave. I figured you were scared of me."

I didn't know what to say, so I didn't say anything. I could feel Georgie watching me real close.

"Have you seen the mother cat?" Kyler asked.

"Not today."

"I'm worried about the littlest one," Kyler said. He pointed to Teacup.

"Me too." I turned my attention back to him. "Do you think it'd be okay if I picked her up?"

Kyler shrugged.

I worried about it for a few moments—was a kitten like a baby bird fallen from its nest? Was I not supposed to touch

Teacup? But I figured since we were petting the other ones, it would be okay.

Teacup felt like she weighed next to nothing. She meowed the tiniest meow I'd ever heard. It was like she was too weak to wriggle around. Even too weak to make much of a noise at all. Too weak to do anything. She seemed worn out. She really did. Eventually, she squirmed her little sausage body a smidge, and her little, nearly toothpick ribs moved under her skin. I scratched her tiny head. Her little ears were flat against her head, not stuck up and out like the other cats. Her eyes moved beneath her paper-thin eyelids, but they still weren't open yet.

"The other kittens' eyes are open," I said.

"Yeah." Kyler said. He came a little closer and watched me pet her. "I actually brought something I wanted to try."

"What's that?"

He pulled an eyedropper-looking thing from his hoodie pocket. "I washed it out and rinsed it really good. It's from ear drops for swimmer's ear. But I watched a video on the internet about it, and . . . " He pulled out something from his jeans pocket. A plastic baggy that looked like it was filled with actual snot.

"Ew," Georgie said.

"It's a raw egg," Kyler explained. "This article said that undernourished kittens might like to eat egg yolk or Karo syrup."

"What's Karo syrup?" George asked.

"It's sugary stuff, a lot like pancake syrup."

"Here," I said. "I'll put Teacup down so you can maybe feed her, or try at least?"

Kyler nodded, and I gently put Teacup down onto the gym shorts. The other kittens were all over Kyler now, probably sniffing at the egg yolk. Kyler sat cross-legged and lifted Teacup in one of his enormous palms. The other kittens purred and rubbed at Kyler's back and knees.

George strained in my grip, trying to get closer to see what Kyler was doing, but I wouldn't let go of his hoodie.

"I just want to see." He drew out the last word for, like, twelve syllables.

"Stay put, George. We forgot our masks. Six feet, remember?"

"The virus is scary," Georgie told Kyler.

Kyler nodded. "It really is. My mom works at the hospital."

"Is she a nurse?" I asked.

"A janitor."

"Where do you live?" George asked.

"On the other side of the Scrub." Kyler had the dropper full of egg yolk now, and he was dragging it over Teacup's mouth and lips. I could tell he was trying to get her interested in eating, but she didn't seem to care. She didn't react.

She did seem to like the crook of Kyler's arm, though. She snuggled more into it.

Kyler tried again and again with the dropper, but Teacup

didn't do as much as lick her lips, or open up her mouth even a smidge for him. Kyler hummed a little, trying one last time.

"Maybe tomorrow I'll bring some Karo syrup," he said finally.

"Can we come back tomorrow?" Georgie asked me. He was playing with one of the black-and-white twins, dragging a piece of straw back and forth on the ground. Mustache put his head low to the ground, wiggled his little butt, and then pounced on the straw, sending Georgie into a fit of giggles each time.

I shook my head. "George, you know we can't come back."

Kyler fixed me with a look. "I could be gone by a certain time if you want to visit the kittens without me being here," he offered.

"It's not you," I explained. "It's that we aren't supposed to be here—I got in trouble for lying and stuff."

"Oh, I get it," Kyler said.

"Plus, True is kind of scared of you," George offered. "From the thing with Derek Sullivan."

"George!"

Kyler's face kind of fell then, along with his shoulders. And his mouth pressed into a flat line.

I said, "I'm sorry," at the same time Kyler said, "I figured."

Kyler wouldn't meet my gaze. He snuggled the tiny runt of a kitten, petted her head gently, even placed a kiss on her forehead. Then, he placed Teacup right in the center of the

quilt nest where the other kittens had been sleeping before. I liked that he did that. I wanted to think her brothers would take care of Teacup, keep her warm.

"It was Dakota Sullivan, not Derek," Kyler said, standing up and moving a bit away from us.

"And you knocked his tooth out," George offered.

"There's two sides to every story," Kyler said with a heavy sigh. "But I did."

"'Cause you're ginormous," Georgie answered. One of the black-and-white kittens perched on George's left shoulder, biting at his dark curly hair.

"Well, I *am* ginormous, I've been told."

Kyler looked at me, and I wasn't sure if I should smile at his joke or not. But I did. He seemed to smile back at me, at least his eyes above his mask scrunched up at the corners.

George wrestled with the kittens, and my map dropped out of Georgie's hoodie pocket.

Kyler picked it up and unrolled it. "Do you mind?" he asked Georgie.

"Aye, aye."

Kyler looked at me.

I translated, "It's pirate talk for 'Yes, go ahead.'"

George lay flat on his back, and Eyepatch sat on his chest, still attacking his curls, tickling George in the process. Mr. Orange strolled over to me and sat in my lap.

Kyler inspected the map, and I watched his face as he did. Was he going to make fun of it? My most recent hand-drawn masterpiece? I felt a fierce stab of protectiveness. I wanted to bundle up that map, Georgie, and little Teacup and run out of here.

But I waited.

Kyler studied the map closely. Then, finally, he looked at Georgie. "You made this?"

"No, no. I wish! True did. Our mom makes maps for real. True's name is a map word. You know, 'true north'?"

"That's your name—True North?" Kyler asked me.

"Yep. It means, like, a fixed point, something that always stays true, even in a spinning world," I explained. I was babbling, because Kyler was studying my map. Hard.

"Hmm." He made a few noises as he took it in, taking forever. Then, he looked up at me. "This is really super cool. Like something you'd see on the inside of a very interesting book."

I felt my cheeks heat at that. I opened my mouth to mutter thanks, and I reached out my hand to grab the map, because . . . I wasn't sure why exactly. It seemed too private.

Just then, I heard the mother cat growl even before I saw her appear from behind several bales of hay. Her tone was low and throaty, and her tail had puffed up in a warning.

"There you are," Kyler said to Mama Cat, adding casually, "Stop with the attitude."

But she ignored Kyler and his easy way. She faced Georgie, who was on all fours with both the black-and-white kittens on his back.

It happened really fast.

Mama Cat hissed and then jumped at Georgie, swatting with one of her paws outstretched. Even from where I was I could see her claws out.

Before I knew it, they were all three rolling in a ball—Georgie, Mama Cat, and Kyler Grier—with Georgie yelping and screaming, the cat hissing, and Kyler's booming voice, yelling, "Calm down, I got her!"

For a heartbeat, I was scared they'd all roll right off the hayloft edge. But then, just like that, it was over.

Kyler pulled himself from Georgie's limbs and stood up. For a second, George still rolled around, swatting at an imaginary foe. Kyler had Mama Cat by the scruff of her neck, and he took her toward the babies' nest. Kyler's chest huffed and puffed with his breathing. He dropped her on the quilt next to Teacup.

"You stay put. No more of that."

Both Mustache and Eyepatch meowed. They quickly joined their mama in the nest. Mr. Orange left my lap too. They all settled down, like it was nothing, but I could still see Mama Cat eyeing George. She looked up at Kyler once, and I swear she was giving him the skunk eye.

"You two should go down the ladder," Kyler said. "I'll watch the mama. She's just being protective."

I was about to thank Kyler, grab Georgie by his own scruff, and get out of there, when another voice boomed loud in the open space of the barn.

"I seen your bike! Come down here, you trespasser!"

Kyler's eyes caught mine, and Georgie scrambled over to me.

"Oh, shoot—it's Old Man Parker," Kyler whispered.

"What should we d—"

Kyler interrupted me, holding his finger to his lips. "He's old and mean, and really . . . let me . . . Just stay here."

Before I could protest, Kyler gave Mama Cat a silent warning with his eyes and one wagging finger, and then he made for the ladder.

I noticed Teacup wasn't inside the quilt nest anymore. Mama was there. Mustache and Eyepatch were there. Mr. Orange too. But Teacup was back on top of the gym shorts, curved into a tiny, pathetic circle, all matted black fur, crinkled whiskers, and tiny ribs poking out.

But we didn't have time for that worry now. I whispered to George to be super quiet *or else*.

"It's me, Mr. Parker," Kyler said, as he hopped down the ladder.

Georgie and I quickly lay on our stomachs and looked over the ledge of the hayloft, trying to stay hidden, yet wanting to see what was going on.

"I told you to stay away from them kittens, boy," the old man said. His gray hair stuck out in all directions, and he wore dirty, faded overalls. "I don't have any use for you here. No odd jobs, no nothing. And you need to return my metal detector. I seen that it was gone. I'm going to the authorities if it isn't back here by tomorrow morning, you understand?"

My cheeks turned hot. I looked to see Georgie's wide stare. He pointed at the corner off by the east eaves where we had left the metal detector.

"Yessir," Kyler told the old man. "I understand."

"I don't condone stealing." Old Man Parker had one missing front tooth, and he lisped on his "s."

"Yessir," Kyler answered.

"That old cat up there, she's mean. You watch yourself. Now get gone."

"I think she has an infection or something in her paw, and I—"

"Nothing doing. I'm done talking with you!"

"Yessir."

Kyler went for the door, and I watched as he turned and looked up at the hayloft, his eyes telling me clearly, *Stay put.*

I wasn't going anywhere.

Old Mr. Parker called out to Kyler, his voice a tiny bit softer. "You done a good job fixing that hayloft ladder. If I need some help anytime soon, I'll let you know."

Huh, the last rung wasn't broken anymore when we came up, was it?

Kyler nodded to Mr. Parker, then he left, and I felt Georgie stiffen next to me.

"We'll wait for the old man to leave, then we'll sneak out." I sounded a lot more calm than I was.

"Why'd Kyler take the blame for us?" Georgie asked.

I shook my head. *Who knew?*

"I thought you said Kyler was mean."

I shrugged. I brought my finger up to my lips. "Shh."

"What if the old man comes up here to check on the kittens?"

"He won't." *I hope.*

We stayed quiet and still, flat on our stomachs, even while Mr. Orange crawled onto Georgie's back and started to bite at his hair.

Finally, the old man put away more and more of his tools, and after several trips to his old pickup outside the barn and then back inside, he got into his truck and left. The crunch of his tires on the gravel was a welcome sound. I let out a huge sigh and sat up, stretching out my poor neck.

Georgie did the same.

"That was a close one," I said.

"I thought you said Kyler was a bad kid—a bully or something."

But I was looking at Teacup. The other kittens were nursing on the mama now, but not Teacup. She just lay there, alone, tiny. It was almost like she didn't have a mom.

I hated the sight of it.

"We better go," Georgie said, tugging at my sleeve.

I thought about pocketing Teacup, taking her home and trying to feed her some Karo syrup or whatever Kyler had been talking about. I could look it up online. Or maybe I could ask Rosie for help because she knew a lot about animals, on account of all of her volunteering at the Cherry Hill Stables. I think they even had barn cats there.

Georgie pulled harder on my sleeve. "Come on. Before the old man gets back."

"Okay, okay."

I couldn't make up my mind about Teacup. Take her? Leave her? She was so little. So lonely.

I stood there, paralyzed. I eventually bent to pick her up. I could just tuck her into the crook of my arm and take off. I could hide her in our basement, maybe? In the shed behind the chicken coop?

But then I froze. I didn't pick up the kitten.

I heard Georgie snuffle a little bit, his breathing sounding wet and a bit aggravated. He rubbed at his nose.

Dad would freak about the kitten if I brought it home. Grandma Jo too. They'd know we'd gone back to the barn. I rubbed my knuckles against my lip and tried to decide. Could a cat carry the virus? Or rabies? Either way, Dad would flip because of George's asthma.

"True!" George yelped. "Gram has gotta miss us by now! We need to go."

"Okay, okay. Alright already."

"Plus, I gotta pee." Georgie danced around a little, crossing his legs this way and that.

"Georgie!" I barked. "Give me just one second."

I pressed a kiss to my fingers, and then I pressed my fingers to little Teacup's forehead.

I left her. I just left her there.

For better. For worse.

Georgie and I went down the ladder, and he carried the metal detector right over to where we'd found it with the other tools.

"I didn't think this barn belonged to anyone," I told George.

"Well, we were wrong about that," he said, in a totally not-helpful way.

We were a few paces into the Scrub when Georgie looked up and sighed. "I really wanted to keep that metal detector."

"I know."

"But I don't want Kyler getting in trouble."

"Yeah."

"It was the best treasure hunt I've ever been on."

I tried to give Georgie a smile. I did. But all I could really think about was Teacup's little poking-out ribs. Her see-through eyelids.

I should've taken her.

"Can we come back tomorrow?"

"Georgie, I don't know . . . "

"I can't hold it anymore, True." Suddenly, he really was doing the potty-dance.

"Go in the bushes over there," I said, pointing toward the creek.

"Okay, don't leave me."

"Georgie, I'm not leaving you, just hurry it up!"

My phone buzzed in my pocket. I took it out. It was a text from Grandma Jo.

You went back to the barn, didn't you?

You're GROUNDED.

Chapter 5

>>>———> 🏠 <———<<<

"You think the rules don't apply to you, True!"

Grandma Jo was super angry with me.

"I'm sorry."

"The thing is, you're not sorry!" she said. I knew I was in serious trouble when she put down her magic-mic—the little device that she held to her throat to make her voice work now that she didn't have a voice box—and grabbed the small whiteboard off the refrigerator.

Sometimes, especially when I was in trouble, Grandma Jo found it easier to yell through her writing.

I stood in the kitchen, my socks wet from the mucky forest, my hands still shaking from almost being caught by Old Man Parker. The thing was, I wasn't really that worried about my punishment from Gram. Or any of this getting-caught business.

I couldn't quit thinking about Teacup.

Georgie peeked in from the family room, raising his eyebrows as if to ask if he should come back in.

I shook my head. *Not yet.*

Rosie walked in and glanced at Grandma Jo writing furiously on the whiteboard. "What did you do?" Rosie asked.

I didn't answer her. Just glared. *Now* she wanted to care about what I was up to? *Now*, when I had completely moved out of our room, like, a month ago? I mean, clothes, desk, everything, right into George's room, and she hadn't said a word.

Rosie must've seen something on the whiteboard she didn't like. She pointed her finger at me. "Did you go somewhere? Did you break the rules?" She waited for me to answer, but I pretended I didn't hear her.

She kept going, "Why aren't you following the rules, True? We can't give Gram the virus, or little Georgie with his asthma! You are being totally selfish!"

My cheeks heated, and my blood felt like it was boiling, but I didn't say anything. I didn't think I had done anything that would put anyone in danger. We hadn't been too close to Kyler, just the kittens. That was okay, wasn't it?

I didn't have time to think it over because Gram handed me the whiteboard.

You think that you can do what you want, that you are smarter than the rules. Let me tell you something, True. You are very smart, but sometimes grown-ups have rules for a reason.

Unlike Georgie—who was now at my side apologizing profusely and telling Rose that we didn't do anything bad and not to tell Dad and please don't make him clean out the chicken coop—I knew when to simply shut up and take my punishment. There was nothing to be discussed right now. Maybe with Mom or Dad. But not Grandma Jo. She scared me.

"Yes, ma'am," I said to Grandma. "I'm sorry."

She scribbled one more line on the whiteboard. *Chicken coop cleanup for a month.*

Go, she mouthed. She pointed up the stairs.

"She gets dinner though, right?" Georgie was still yapping. "Her tummy will hurt without dinner."

I didn't hang around to hear the rest of Georgie's defense of me. I hoped he wouldn't spill all the beans though. I hoped he wouldn't let them know that we had seen Kyler or the kittens, because Gram knowing we were at the barn . . . well, that was bad enough.

Plus, if I was telling the truth, I was already thinking about when I could get back there to check on little Teacup.

I sat down at Georgie's and my partner desk, and I muttered under my breath. "Yes, ma'am. Grown-ups know everything. I understand. I'm nothing. Got it."

I clicked on the old desktop computer that Georgie and I shared for e-learning. I logged into my email—not my school email but my regular email—because I knew Mom would've sent me a message.

I hadn't picked up the last three nights when she had tried to video chat with me. I was still so . . . angry.

While the ancient computer heated up, I pulled a map that

I had made for Georgie off his bulletin board, the one showing Minnesota and the lower portion of Canada.

Mom was in Manitoba. Only 342 miles away.

It might as well have been a thousand miles. A million.

She had promised she'd be home this weekend. As soon as her quarantine was over. And the guy on her team who had the virus wasn't even really sick! Just barely.

This was Mom's longest trip yet, even without the extra quarantine time. Every time she was about to go somewhere for work, I would draw a map to show Georgie exactly where she was going to be. It seemed closer to see it drawn that way. She seemed closer.

She liked to tell Georgie that even when she was traveling for work, she was there in spirit, right next to him, like a hummingbird hovering over his shoulder, whispering in his ear how much she loved him.

She used to tell me the hummingbird thing too when I was little and she went away. Now, she probably expected me to be too grown-up for that kind of thing. But I still liked it.

I missed Mom.

The way she smelled. The way she said "lift" instead of "elevator." The way her laugh sounded like a jingle bell. The way she moved her hands when she worked on a map. All sure and quick. She hummed when she worked on her maps, too, mostly old Beatles songs.

I missed her funny sense of humor, the way she liked when I was bossy, how she corrected people and said,

"Pishposh, True's not bossy at all, I call it *leadership*." I missed the way she rolled her eyes when I would do maps in miles. "When the entire rest of the world uses kilometers, I cannot see why my own progeny has to be so very American." She had winked when she said that, of course.

When she was gone with her job, our whole house seemed deflated, like a balloon after a party. Just not as much fun.

My email popped up on the computer screen, and sure enough, I had one unread message from Mom.

Dear Daughter,

In your eleven years, you have lived up to your name—True North. You always know what's right, and you are brave, strong, true. I know you're angry. I wish you'd talk to me. This is a scary time, for all of us. Being angry at me might feel better than being scared or worried. Think about that. Why is that?

And I'm here, ready to talk, whether on email or hopefully on the phone, when you're ready, luv.

Mom

My throat tingled. My nose itched. My eyes stung. I didn't want to cry, so I closed that email fast, and I opened up a web browser and typed in "how to help a tiny kitten." I skimmed through a few articles but didn't find too much helpful info.

Then I tried, "how to help save a runt."

I read a couple of the web pages, and each article kind of

said the same thing, that it was really up to the mother cat, and that she would do what was right. But I wanted to know what to do if the mother wasn't up for the job.

So I typed, "why won't a mom feed her kitten?"

"Are you going to sneak back there and check on the kittens?" It was Georgie, all snot-nosed and scaring me half to death. I hadn't even known he had come in the room.

"No, I'm not," I told him. I crossed my fingers over the keyboard when I said it. Another lie. But he couldn't come with me. Not this time.

I closed out the window on the computer and turned toward Georgie.

"I wanted that metal detector."

"George, really? We barely scraped by without getting every privilege we ever had taken away, and you're complaining about not getting to keep that darn old metal detector? Stop being a baby."

"I'm not a baby."

"Then don't act like one."

Of course, Rose chose that moment to appear in the doorway. "Quit being mean to Georgie."

"Mind your own business," I snapped.

"I just finished talking to Mom on the phone. She would like to talk to you."

I shook my head.

"Seriously, True?"

I didn't answer.

"You know what? You are unbelievable, True. The whole world is a mess. We are in a pandemic, you know? You think you could quit thinking about yourself all the time, and not . . . I don't know."

"I am not always thinking about myself," I said.

"People are dying, True. There's a kid in my class whose cousin in Trevor County has it. Like, for real. People get it, and for people who already have other things wrong with their health . . . well, it can be super serious."

"But Tamsin told me other kids are getting to see each other now that the shelter-in-place is lifted. They can be outside at least. Ride bikes. Go to stores, as long as they wear a mask," I argued.

"I know," Rosie offered. "Dad's just extra cautious because Grandma Jo is healing after her cancer treatments. Plus, Dad sees what's going on at the hospital."

"Well, then maybe Dad doesn't need to know all our details . . . " I gave her a hopeful look.

"True, no way. Listen, you don't remember when Georgie was little. When he had his worst asthma attack. It was terrifying—his skin turned this blue-green color 'cause he couldn't breathe. It really and truly freaked me out. Bad things don't only happen to other people, True. We're not, like, living some charmed, fairy-tale life. You're old enough to understand that. So quit being selfish."

"Fine," I muttered, staring at the map of Canada on my

desk. Why couldn't Mom just come home and even out all the rough edges of this house and all of us in it?

But Rosie didn't stop. She kept talking, scaring me with statistics and stories and all kinds of stuff. Georgie was probably terrified.

I wanted to cry more than ever, because I didn't want to think about what was going on in the world or Georgie getting hurt. Or death.

I had a sudden urge to fling myself into Rosie's arms. Just stand up from the computer and throw my arms around her waist and admit that I *was* scared. I could picture it. A year ago, even a few months ago, I would've done it.

But now, I don't know. She was so far away.

I wanted how we used to be. Close. I loved how I would run to her bed when I felt scared at night, and she would toss her arm around me and cuddle me, and it was just me and Rosie against the world. She would hum Beatles songs until I fell asleep.

I wanted to tell her what was going on with me. What was out at the barn. What had happened.

I wanted her to tell me what to do about Teacup.

I wanted to talk to her.

I wanted her to be sad that I'd moved out of our room.

I wanted her to still want to do the Sister-Skate-a-Thon fundraiser with me. But when it got canceled because of the virus, she seemed relieved not to have to do it.

I missed Rosie.

I missed Mom.

I missed them both so much.

Rosie still stood in our bedroom doorway, and she'd narrowed her eyes at me. She was so crabby with me. Before, one time when I'd said something to Mom about Rosie, about her not liking me anymore, Mom had said, "Pishposh, True, she's just growing up."

I thought about that now, looking at Rosie scowling at me from the doorway. Didn't Rosie know that her growing up and away from me was breaking my heart in pieces?

I tried hard not to cry. I used all my will to push back the tears. It felt important not to give in, not to crack. I needed this win. There was too much going on, and all I really, really wanted to do was make a plan to save Teacup.

So I calmly stood up, and I walked over to the doorway, and I very slowly shut the door in Rose's face.

"True!"

I ignored her.

I turned to Georgie. I knew how to be a good big sister. I did.

He looked like he was about to side with Rosie and tell me I was being too mean to her, but I didn't give him a chance.

"George, I will make you another map. We don't need a metal detector to look for treasure, you know."

"We don't?"

I heard Rosie make an aggravated noise and stomp away down the hallway. I pretended I didn't hear it.

"No, we don't," I answered George. I rolled out some more of the butcher paper, and I used scissors to cut off a large section, which I spread out on our partner desk. "Get me the good markers."

"Oh, True, thank you! This will be great. Maybe Kyler can help us find the treasure."

"Sorry, buddy, you can't tell anyone that we saw him."

"I can't?"

"Nope. And, well, I'm gonna need your help."

"Aye, aye, Captain!"

🌲 🌲 🌲

"Do you know where he lives?" I asked Tamsin over video chat. "Kyler Grier?"

She answered, "On the east side, of course. In the apartment complex past the trestle. Where all the other poor kids live."

It wasn't that it wasn't true—it was—but why did she have to say it like that? Didn't she know how snotty it sounded?

I was out in the Scrub myself, looking for a good place to bury my compass, so Georgie could come and dig it up. I planned on finishing the map tonight and taking George out tomorrow morning. My leash was pretty short, but miraculously Gram had let me come out here after dinner. I mean, she thought I was back by the fence cutting some basil for the kitchen and feeding the chickens, but . . . let's just say it worked out for me that Gram slept a lot still. Catnaps here and there. She was still recovering, Dad always told us.

Tamsin's brows turned down on my phone screen. "Why are you asking me about Kyler Grier anyway?"

I shrugged. "No reason."

"You know he was the one who knocked out Derek Sullivan's tooth."

"It was Dakota Sullivan's tooth," I snapped. "And, yes, I know what Kyler did. Everyone's told me about it. Including him."

"When did you see him?"

"I ran into him. It wasn't—"

"Where'd you run into him? You're not supposed to go anywhere!"

"It was in the Scrub by the—"

"True! He probably *has it.* You know? His mom works at the hospital, like, as a janitor or something. Did he cough?"

"My dad works at the hospital."

"Well, yeah, but he's a doctor."

"A nurse."

"Yeah."

My temper stirred, like a snake about to strike, and there was too much going on in my world right now. I didn't want to have a big fight with Tamsin. Sometimes she could be so . . . *ugh.*

"Hey, I should go."

"Do you know anyone who has it?" she asked.

"No. Um, Rosie does though. Some kid in Trevor County."

"Listen, True, I'm sorry about your mom and everything. I know this is hard for you. Hey, send me a pic of that new map when you finish it for Georgie."

"I will. And guess what? Gram let me order the next Percy Jackson."

"Cool, I'll order it too! We'll read it together over video. Can we?"

"We can."

I hung up the call and pocketed my phone. Then, I dug a deep hole beneath a weeping willow on the edge of the creek bed and buried the compass. George would be able to find it easily, I figured. The tree was a good landmark. I would be able to draw the willow easily enough too.

I pulled out my phone and looked at the time.

I could probably get to the other side of the Scrub and back before Gram would miss me. At least I hoped that was true.

Maybe.

If I ran.

I quickly fed the chickens, refilled their water, wiped my hands on my jeans, and I took off.

Chapter 6

I was sweaty and worn out by the time I got to the apartment complex near the library. I didn't really know what to do once I got there. It was a set of four three-story buildings with an entry door and a stoop leading to each individual building. They were plain and squat-looking, like they'd been made from Legos and painted the ugliest gray anyone could find.

Part of me was tugging to go home. Reminding me I shouldn't be here. But at the same time, it felt a little thrilling to know that I chose to be here, even if I was teetering on the brink of getting in serious trouble.

Some trash tumbled along the parking lot asphalt as the wind blew: a few fast-food wrappers, an old, white baby sock, a yellow spork. I kicked those around a while, and I tried to figure out a plan. How could I find out which apartment Kyler was in?

I chose the closest building and went inside. I looked at the last names listed next to the buzzers for the intercoms, but I didn't find Grier.

Okay. On to the next building.

Same thing. No Grier on the buzzers.

Three little kids played on the stoop at the farthest apartment building. It was starting to get a tiny bit dark, so I had to do something fast. I walked over toward them. I slipped a paper mask from my pocket.

As I was putting it on, I saw a large figure come out of the apartment building. He said hi to the kids playing on the stoop, laughed about something with them that I couldn't quite hear. He started toward the road, away from me, but then, figuring it had to be him, I called out his name.

"Kyler!" My voice sounded rusty and unsure.

He stopped and turned. I waved and trotted toward him. He waved back and came toward me.

We both stopped a good ten or twelve feet away from the other one. I raised my hand and waved at him again. This lockdown was making me weird.

He was already wearing his mask. It made me think of Georgie's teacher who, the other day during one of his e-learning classes, said that wearing masks during this time was how we show we care for others.

"Hey, True." Kyler said it like it wasn't bonkers that I had chased him down in the parking lot. He said it like we were maybe friends—ones that saw each other in the halls at Spooner Middle and waved.

Why weren't we? Why couldn't we be?

Just because his gym shoes were super old and he wore the same two hoodies every other day?

No, there was more to it than that. I knew that. Right?

"First, I wanted to say thanks for not turning in George and me to Old Man Parker."

He nodded. "And second?"

"Why did you knock Dakota Sullivan's tooth out?"

He let out a breath like he had been waiting for me to ask that exact question. "Well," he said, rubbing the back of his neck, "the short answer is because I lost my temper."

"I can relate to that."

"But the real answer is that as soon as I moved here, as soon as I move anywhere, someone gets it in their head to make fun of my size. And they pick at me. You know the type: the Sullivan twins and their friends, especially Miles McAlvoy. You know what I'm saying?"

I did know. Tamsin lived next door to Miles McAlvoy. She loved the way his hair curled up off his forehead and was forever calling him cute. But he wasn't always the nicest. It was Peter McAlvoy—Miles's brother—who gave Georgie the unfortunate nickname of "Diaper Baby" after his little accident in kindergarten.

"So you're telling me Dakota Sullivan deserved it? That I shouldn't think you're some big bully?"

Kyler rolled his eyes. "I'm not telling you to do anything. I'm just answering your question. They teased me and kept taking my calculator from my locker so I wouldn't have it for math. One time they told the teacher that I was too poor to have a calculator and could they set up a fundraiser to get me one?" Kyler made a frustrated noise and started pacing. "This was all in, like, the first three days of living here, you know? Then nobody would come near me or say hi or anything, because those guys kept poking at me, you know? And I've moved a lot. I knew . . . I *knew*, there was no getting rid of them unless . . . "

"Unless you clocked one of them."

"Exactly."

"Well, you did. And now everyone's scared of you."

"Yup." The look in Kyler Grier's eyes was so sad. Something under my ribs pinched.

"My gram says sometimes you have to stick up for yourself or nobody will respect you."

"Yeah, I guess."

"Is that what you were doing?"

"I suppose."

I put my hands on my hips and studied Kyler, narrowing my eyes at him. He stared right back at me. A challenge. I didn't want to just let him off the hook, but what he said made a whole lot of sense. I'd seen firsthand what snakes that group of boys could be, with their relentless teasing and bullying.

Kyler's gaze fell from mine, and he brought both his fists up to his eyes and rubbed them real hard. His voice got so low, just a whisper. "I threw up behind the school dumpster after I hit him, you know. I felt so horrible about the whole thing."

He did?

I took a step closer, reached my hand out to him, then without thinking, I patted him on the shoulder kind of awkward-like. "It's okay, really. . . . I get it, Kyler. Sometimes you have to let people know you're tough, and—"

Kyler wiped his eyes with the edge of his sleeve. He said something, but I missed it because of the mask. He sat down on the curb. I followed him.

"What did you say?" I asked. Was he actually crying?

"I just said, sometimes I wish I didn't have to be."

"Didn't have to be what?"

"Tough."

"Tough?"

"Yeah."

I thought about that. I really thought about it, as I sat on that dirty old curb next to Kyler, staring out into the apartment parking lot.

Kyler Grier surprised me.

He was three times the size of every other fifth grader in Spooner Middle. He could flatten every last one of those jerks. If I had come here for some kind of answer or explanation, I'd gotten it. But I still didn't know what to say exactly. I think Kyler was more complicated than people wanted him to be. Maybe we all were.

So I only nodded.

And then Kyler told me lots of things, how he saw me drawing a map in social studies class in February, right before the lockdown, and how he thought it was the coolest thing he'd ever seen, and he wanted to tell me but felt too shy.

He told me about how he wanted to join the engineering club at school and build bridges out of popsicle sticks, but he was too scared because one of McAlvoy's friends was in it, the one with the long hair.

I told him that was Fitz. He was the worst of them.

Then Kyler told me he had a big, fuzzy cat named Hobbes, who had a totally grumpy attitude—even for a cat.

He told me about these cool new books he'd gotten at the library—the Dragonmyth Saga. He'd started the series right after he finished—*finished!*—the entire Percy Jackson series.

He actually ran inside to his apartment to grab the first Dragonmyth book, just to show me the map on the inside cover.

"Wow," I told him. "Look at the gold shiny stuff on this thing."

"I know. Do you maybe want to borrow it, before I take it back to the library?"

"Sure! I'd love to read it." I traced my finger over the different places on the map. *The Feathered Forest. The Slickest Sea. The Horn-Winged Bramble.* The calligraphy was amazing, with tiny hidden creatures within the letters themselves, the "l" in Bramble curling into a long, spiked tail. The detail was incredible. I already wanted to know what story this map told. I couldn't wait to read this book—it was a perfect fit for me. And suddenly, I felt shy, like I couldn't quite meet Kyler's eyes.

"Thanks," I said.

"I have the second one too, but I'm not done with it yet."

I nodded. "Oh figs!" I looked at my phone, realizing I was certainly taking way too long out in the Scrub for Grandma Jo's liking. "I have to get going. I'm kind of grounded. But, um . . . " I stood up and brushed off the seat of my pants. "I'm worrying about Teacup—the runt. I wanted to, um, check on her."

"You want to meet at the barn tomorrow after e-learning?"

"Yeah." I met his eyes.

He didn't look so sad anymore. "Okay, True. I'll see you then?"

I thought about all the reasons I shouldn't go.

But I nodded anyway. He nodded too. The crinkles by his eyes told me he was smiling beneath his mask.

"I'll meet you after school," I said.

I took off running.

Tomorrow!

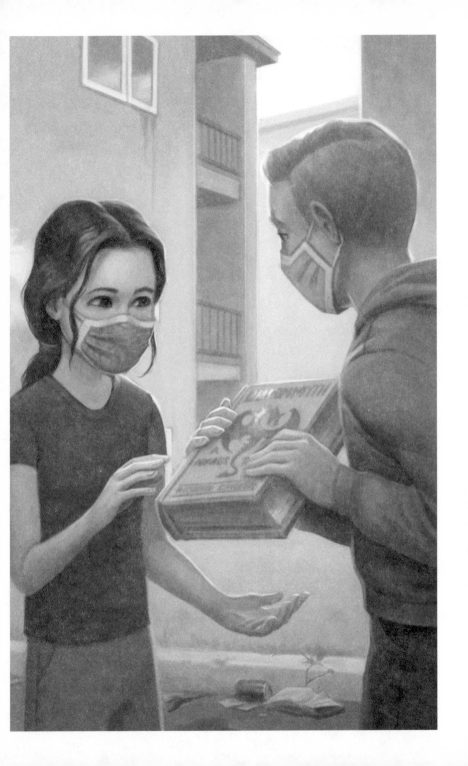

Chapter 7

True Vincent

5th grade/Mrs. Burns block 2

Creative writing assignment

Remote e-learning day 30

Lesson 3: Symbols
The Map Legend

Maps should be smaller versions of a place or a subject that represents a huge, sprawling, ginormous place. So, instead of putting in all the details, sometimes you have to choose a symbol to represent something.

And that can be a lot of fun. For instance, when I was drawing a map of Tamsin's house, I used a pickle as the symbol for her room. Because—and don't tell anyone—her mother calls her "Pickle." It's like her pet name.

You can use symbols that make sense to almost everyone, like a stop sign or a railroad track. But you can choose symbols to be like your kinda sorta secret, too, and then it's like a special buried code in your map.

I do this all the time in my maps. I like to draw maps that when you fold them a certain way, there is a special message inside. I made one for Georgie that, when you folded it, said, "Oh figs!"

So go forth! Use some symbols. Hide some secrets!

♠ ♣ ♠

"Check around the stump."

"Aye, aye." Georgie crawled on his hands and knees around the stump. "The map has the X on the southwest side."

"George Bacon Vincent, Mom is going to love how you're learning your directions."

Georgie went still at Mom's name, and I worried I'd ruined the spell of this treasure hunt.

But he moved on. "I think it's here." He started to dig with his hands.

This map had Georgie not only finding a super-great treasure at the end, but also digging up pieces of the map itself along the way—like a homemade jigsaw puzzle. It'd taken me a while to bury all the pieces of the map, but oh, this was a good one. Mom would love to hear about it.

If I ever got around to emailing her.

George quickly found the piece of paper. It was the corner piece, the one that would take him near the snake hole by the bramble bushes that always scraped our ankles.

He lifted up the map piece and shook the dirt from it. He

studied it for a long moment before he turned it right side up, north at the top. I couldn't help but smile.

"Blimey, this is a tough hunt! Onward to the bramble bushes!"

"Batten down the hatches!" I didn't really know what that meant, but Georgie said it all the time.

"Why did I have to bring a mask?" Georgie asked as we neared the bushes.

"A surprise. Now come on, lazy. You only have one more stop, and you are going to *love* it."

George quickly dug up the next map piece, and he easily figured out that the next and last stop was at the concrete block that stuck high out of the creek bed. Near the willow tree. But before he moved on, he laid each map piece together, flat on the dirt floor of the Scrub.

"I love that you made this for me." He looked up at me and smiled. His nose was running.

"Wipe your nose, kid."

"I think I want to give you a hug."

"If you have to," I joked.

He ran into my arms and gave me a real squeezer. "I like hugging you, True."

"Same, Georgie." We started walking toward the willow tree, and George grabbed my hand.

"Benny in my kindergarten class is funny on Zoom, but he's funnier in class. And he always shares his yogurt raisins at lunch."

"You'll see him soon, I bet."

"Isn't it weird to be scared of touching and seeing other people?"

For some reason, I thought of Kyler. "Who are you scared of?"

"No one. Everyone."

"You mean because of the virus?"

He nodded. "Do you think we'll ever go back to school?"

"Yes, we will."

"But when?"

We had made it to the willow tree.

"I thought it would be before now," I admitted. "It's just taking a long time."

"I heard Dad coughing last night in the basement. He doesn't have it, does he?"

"No, Georgie."

"Is this where I dig? The X looks like it's on the eastern side, like right here." He kicked at the concrete block. Right by where I had dug that morning. Very deep. This was the treasure. And boy, it was a good one.

"You are right on point, Georgie. You better get digging."

"I hope it's a puppy."

"It's not a puppy."

"That was a joke, True."

"Right. You know, you'll have to make me a map next."

George stopped digging abruptly. "I will?"

"Why not?"

"I bet I could do it. I'm not a baby anymore, you know." It was like he'd never even considered the idea before. He looked thrilled. I was even more excited about that than I was for him to find his treasure. He kept talking, "True, I want to make a map, but how do I start? What should—"

"Actually, I've been working on something at school, in creative writing class, like a whole how-to book on mapmaking. I think I've been making it for you without realizing it was for you. I'll help you."

He laughed. "I just never thought . . . " He laughed again.

"Never thought what?"

"That I could be big like you."

I smiled and rolled my eyes. "We all grow up, Georgie." For some reason, I thought of Rosie. Of how she turned into a teenager in a snap of the fingers, or at least it felt that way. It made me think of Tamsin and her obsessive talk about Miles McAlvoy. "Don't grow up too fast, buddy."

"I won't," he answered solemnly. "Um, True? After this treasure hunt, I mean, if you think it's okay, do you think we could, um, maybe . . . "

"George?"

"What?"

"Do you see what is blowing the *winds of change* in the corner of your map?"

He looked at the different pieces of his map. "Um . . . cats? That's weird, True. Even for you."

94

"No, I'm trying to tell you something. It's a symbol for a secret—"

"Oh my gosh! Yes! That's what I was trying to ask. I wanted to know—"

"I know, goof. And yes, sir. We are going to check on the kittens. But it has to be our secret. 'Cause I'm still all kinds of grounded."

"Pirate Promise." He did his homemade salute, and then returned to the map. A moment later, he was uncovering his treasure. "Oh my gosh. No way. Absolutely no way."

He removed the paper towel I'd wrapped around the compass to protect it. He peered closely at the treasure, bringing it right up to his nose. He rubbed it on his shirt.

"No way. I can't believe it. You are giving me your compass!"

"It's Mom's compass, given to her by her father. It's the Vincent family compass, just on loan to the newest mapmaker."

His eyes sparkled, and he lifted the compass right up to his nose. I figured he was probably studying the super-fancy dragons engraved on the brass cover, but then Georgie brought that thing right to his lips and gave it a big smooch.

I couldn't help myself—I laughed. I nearly grabbed him to give him a hug and pinch his chubby little cheeks.

"How's it work?" he asked.

"For now, know that it will always show you which way is north, no matter where you are, so you can't get lost. Not really lost anyway." I showed him how to hold it flat in his hand, and I pointed at the needle. "That needle is a magnet that always points north."

He jumped to his feet and twirled around, keeping the compass in his palm, watching the needle as he spun.

He made me smile. "Jeez, kid, I would've given it to you ages ago if I would've known how much you'd love it."

"You are the best sister there is," he said, and he flung his arms around me. But as soon as I hugged him back, he was already on the move. "To the kittens!"

"To the kittens!"

"They are not north at all. They are"—he looked at his compass—"mostly west, but a little south, too. Onward!"

I ran after him, smiling. But I was also thinking of Rosie, of when she gave that same compass to me and how I'd felt like a million bucks. Like a real grown-up kid. And like I'd never, ever have a better friend than my older sister.

"He's here?" Georgie asked, as we came out of the Scrub.

"Yeah," I answered. I was about to launch into some kind of defense of Kyler, why it was okay he was here, but apparently George didn't need it. He just reached into his pocket and put on his mask. I did the same.

"Look what I got from True!" He ran up to Kyler, but Kyler put out his hands to stop George from getting too close.

"I see. That's really cool. With that compass and a map, you could do anything."

"I can."

Kyler wore a gray hoodie today, but it was as old and threadbare as his other one. Same blue paper mask.

George talked a mile a minute. "It's extra funny because you use a compass to find true north and that's both my sisters' names."

"Oh yeah? What's your other sister's name?"

"Compass Rose."

Kyler looked over at me.

"It's true," I said. "Dad says our mom is *fanciful*." I used air quotes around the words just like Dad always did.

For some reason, that made Kyler smile. "I like it."

"Did you see the kittens yet?" I asked.

"Not yet. I was waiting out here for you. Plus, I hid my bike in the brush behind the barn. In case Mr. Parker comes around."

We walked toward the barn. I had to yank on George's collar to keep him by me and not totally all over Kyler. Apparently social distancing rules were hard when you had some kind of hero worship.

"What's in the backpack?" Kyler asked.

"Lots of stuff," I said "I brought a zillion things for Teacup to try to eat. I read up on it."

"Like what?"

"Like the syrup you talked about. We had it in the pantry.

And I brought a can of tuna, because, I don't know, I just want to see if we can help her eat. Maybe just squeeze the juice of it out on her lips, get her interested."

"You know, I talked to my mom about Teacup."

"Yeah?" I bristled. I didn't want to hear what his mom said, when my mom wasn't around to ask. And I didn't like the way he was just throwing Teacup's name around. I mean, I thought of her as mine.

"She says the mother is supposed to take care of the baby when it's this little, but—"

"I know that," I snapped. "But the mother obviously isn't taking care."

"I told Mr. Parker, too, actually, and—"

"You talked to him after he yelled at us?" George asked, opening and closing his compass, clearly enjoying the little click of the lid as it closed. It was a good sound. A comforting one.

"Yeah, I came to apologize to Mr. Parker, and I had to make sure you returned the metal detector—because I didn't want, you know, trouble from him. Anyway, I ended up clearing out the weeds on his back porch for him 'cause his back isn't so good these days. And I talked to him about the mama cat. He came back here with me and held her so I could look at her paw. I thought she had some kind of infection, but it was just a bad sliver—"

"You got it out?" George asked.

"I did. Mr. Parker had me pour some alcohol on the paw

too, because it looked a little red. Anyway, he thought the runt—"

"Her name's Teacup," I said.

"So Old Man Parker isn't always mean?" George asked.

Kyler shrugged. "He isn't mean exactly all the time. Just . . . grumpy. Did you know he owns six horses, and he has four dogs?"

"He does?" Georgie's eyes lit up.

"Yeah, and the oldest dog has only three legs. And likes to eat pie of all things."

"How did you find that out?" I asked.

"Well, that's a long story."

"I like pie," George announced. "I'm going up!" He made for the ladder.

"Why do you help that grumpy old guy?" I asked Kyler.

Kyler shrugged.

"Seriously. Tell me. Are you hoping he'll let us take the kittens? Or use the barn or—"

"No, it's not that," Kyler answered. He seemed to think for a moment. "I think it's just 'cause since I moved here, I'm . . . lonely." He kicked his shoes around in the dirt of the barn floor.

"Lonely?"

"Yeah. At school, after that Sullivan thing. Then we locked down. I don't have any friends, really. Mr. Parker's alone, too. I don't know . . . " He looked up at me for a second, then looked away quickly. "He seemed to need a friend, and—"

"You're nice!" I blurted.

"Well, you don't have to sound so surprised!" Kyler smiled. I couldn't see it because of his mask, but I heard it, and I saw his eyes crinkle up. And it felt contagious. I smiled too.

Then I remembered something. "Before the lockdown, I thought I saw you at the library. Did I see you there? Were you doing story time for the little kids? I mean, at the time, I thought, 'No way!' But now . . . "

The tips of Kyler's ears went red. "Yeah, it was me."

"You were reading out loud—a book about robots."

"The kids loved that one."

"And then you did a craft with paper plates and tinfoil."

"The librarian lives in my building. She needed help that day, and I like to—"

"Prove people wrong?" I finished.

"Ha!" Kyler let out a bark of laughter, and I did too, but then George yelped.

"Kyler, True! I think you should come up here. I think you should come right now!"

"What is it?" Kyler called.

But I was already moving because I knew Georgie's voice. I knew his panic-style sound. I was up that ladder as fast as possible. And when I got up there, I saw the familiar heap of kittens, just as I had seen them the other day. The three healthy babies all curled up, looking fatter and healthier, their fur shinier.

Mama was wound around them, protecting them, but then I realized Georgie wasn't looking at them. No, he was pointing to the corner.

And in the corner, far under the western eaves, in a pile of cobwebs and crunchy old hay, lay my Teacup. She had curled in on herself, a semicircle, her little ribs, her sausage-body looking so thin, not round at all. Her little nose had no pink left in it but was an eerie white. And when I watched her chest, it didn't move.

"Oh no, oh no, oh no." I was on the floor next to Teacup, and my hand shook as I reached out and petted her little forehead, as gently as I could. In my mind, I was already rushing her home, telling Grandma Jo everything, calling the emergency vet up by the Walgreens on Cedar Road.

Calling Dad at the hospital.

I petted Teacup again, her forehead, down her spine, scratched under her chin, but nothing happened. She didn't squirm. Not at all. Not even a little bit.

I picked her up, oh so very gently. I held her in my hands, and I put her face next to mine, trying to feel a breath.

Nothing.

I placed her in my lap and tried to find a pulse in her neck.

I didn't want to admit it.

"No, no, no. It can't be," I whispered.

I let myself admit that her body was not warm. It wasn't warm at all. Not even a little bit.

Her little eyelids were still closed, sunken in a tiny bit. They would never open. Never see her mama. Never play with her brothers.

I was too late. I should've brought her home the other day. Why hadn't I? I couldn't remember. Had there been reasons?

I wished I could go back and change my decision.

But I couldn't fix this.

This was done. She was gone. Well and truly gone.

I realized then that George stood behind me, leaning onto my shoulders, his voice shaking. "Maybe she's just sleeping real hard, True," he said, his eternally snotty nose running.

And then I realized that someone was crying, big sloppy sobs, big huge baby tears, and it was me.

I was crying in front of George. In front of Kyler.

I held Teacup close to my chest, and I gave her a kiss.

I grabbed Kyler's old gym uniform from near the other kittens' bed, and I used one hand to fold it as nicely as I could, and then laid it on the loft floor. I placed Teacup in the center of her own little nest. I kissed her again. I stroked down her spine.

Once. Twice.

I somehow got down the ladder of the hayloft, and I know that Georgie followed me.

I was in the Scrub in no time, my tears still falling. I ran. I wanted away from there. From what had happened. What I had *let* happen.

My stomach hurt.

I missed my mother.

I thought I might throw up.

I wanted home.

I was a huge ginormous baby who cried.

I wanted my maps and I wanted my bed and I wanted Dad and his big, long sighs. And I wanted Grandma Jo, even though this was all her fault, and Dad's fault, with all their rules and worries, and I wanted Mom even though I was still so mad at her. And I wanted Rose, but not the Rose she was now, the one she used to be.

I wanted everything to rewind. Before the lockdown.

Before things got so hard.

I wanted to draw a map that could show me how to get out of here. To get away from the now.

To lead me away from this. Anywhere that wasn't here.

I wanted a map that could get me away from all this heartbreak. Was there a map that could show me that?

But I knew—I *knew*—it wouldn't be a true map. It would somehow, some way, lead me right back home. It would lead me right back into Georgie's bedroom.

Back to his old desktop computer. Back to our partner desk and my butcher paper. My colored pencils.

Pishposh, I could hear Mom telling me. *The only way out is through.*

I could almost imagine her here, with me, now. Her sweet lemon scent. Her easy way.

I was at our back gate in no time, all tears and muddy

boots, with a crying Georgie at my heels. I suddenly didn't like myself very much.

"Go inside," I told him.

"But what . . . you're . . . "

Suddenly, I knew what I had to do. "I can't just leave her there. I have to go back. I need to bury her in the gym suit. She was mine to take care of, and I—"

"True! You can't just . . . I'm coming with."

I pushed Georgie toward the house. "Get in the house right now, and you tell Gram I'm cleaning out the coop."

Georgie sobbed, and his shoulders drooped. "She was so little."

"I know, George." He grasped me around the waist, wiped his snotty nose on me and snuffled, coughed once, then twice.

"I'll do what you say, but only because I'm tired, True."

I took out his inhaler, gave it to him. He took two puffs.

"Go," I told him.

He nodded, then trudged into the house.

🌲 🌲 🌲

Up in the hayloft, Kyler sat with Teacup in his lap, his eyes red, the gym suit still swaddled around her. Mustache sat in his lap as well, grooming little Teacup's ears.

Kyler didn't seem surprised to see me back. "Her brothers were saying goodbye," he explained. "I figured I'd let them before we dug a hole out back."

I nodded. "I'll grab the shovel."

I looked out at the land behind the barn. I wanted there to be a pretty spot, like sun shining through the trees, daffodils just sprouting from the ground, something good, a sign. But it all just looked like the Scrub. Nothing special.

"Right here's good," I said as Kyler stepped up next to me. It was hard to keep my voice from quavering too much. I yanked on my ponytail and twisted it around my fingers, thinking.

I picked a spot that I thought you could probably see through the slats of the hayloft wall, beneath what I thought were lilac bushes that got all smelly and purple in the summer.

I speared the point of the shovel into the dirt.

Kyler had found a small cardboard box somewhere in the barn and had put Teacup inside. He'd used the Spooner gym suit as bedding, and something about that—that I didn't even have to tell him to do it—pinched at my throat, ached behind my ribs. I had to turn away.

I busied myself digging the hole. Once I had worked up a good sweat, struggling against the claylike soil, Kyler took over without saying a word. He dug the hole a whole bunch deeper with just a few shovelfuls. He was strong.

When he placed the box in the ground, I knelt down next to him. I didn't want him to talk, and it was like he knew. We stayed there in a silent moment for Teacup, and I wiped at my eyes. Sniffled.

Kyler kept silent, clearing his throat a few times. When he stood up to grab the shovel and put the dirt back in, he put his hand on my shoulder for just a second. And it meant to me, in a silent way, like, *I get it, True. I'm sorry.*

We walked back toward the barn. Kyler had a big splotch of dirt on his mask, and one more on his forehead. I was about to tell him when he said, "It's like when I have to move."

"What's like that?"

"It makes me sad."

"It's sadder than that."

Kyler nodded but didn't say anything else.

As I put the shovel back with the other tools, Kyler said, "I just mean it's sad in the same way. An ending. Hard to handle."

I thought about that. That was exactly why this was sad. It was an ending, and I wanted a do-over. I wanted to go back and do something different. Bring Teacup back home with me. *Save her.*

Everything inside me was twisted up and curled into a throbbing fist. Who knew being sad could make you feel so angry? So ready to punch something?

I wanted to kick something hard and cry and scream and throw a Georgie-style tantrum, but that wouldn't bring back that little kitten, would it?

The barn door slid open, and a long slant of late-afternoon sun blinded us both for a second before we brought our hands up to shade our eyes.

"What are you doing here again, boy?" It was Old Man Parker, somehow looking surlier than ever. He coughed into a handkerchief and scowled at us.

"The runt died," Kyler explained.

"I don't care if the runt died. You aren't supposed to be out here, using my tools."

"We aren't, sir."

Suddenly, I couldn't take this old fart being mean to Kyler anymore, not when I knew how nice Kyler was to him, the things he did for him, how he tried to be his friend and look past his super-crabbiness.

I stalked toward the old man and wagged my finger at him. I was shaking all over. "You're awfully mean," I said, "to somebody who seems to help you a whole lot."

The old man sneered at me. "Little girl, are you the one who stole my metal detector?"

That shook me a little, but I wasn't about to apologize right now. "Yeah." I put my hands on my hips. "But I brought it back."

"Stealing is stealing." He narrowed his eyes. "Wait until I tell your Grandma Jo."

His words sent me reeling. "How do you know my grandma?"

"I play bingo with Jo at the senior center, or we used to anyway. You must be the sassy one she always talks about."

"Please don't tell her." I was shaking with both anger and

fear now, my knees knocking, my whole body feeling like a cocked fist.

He turned to Kyler. "You bury the runt in the back?"

Kyler nodded. "Yessir."

"You let Teacup die," I spat at Mr. Parker. "This is your barn. You should've saved her."

When the old man looked back at me, it wasn't with his regular mean snarl anymore, but rather with some softness to his face. He took a step toward me. But I couldn't take it. Not his niceness. Not sympathy.

No way.

I ran out the barn door, my legs working hard, my lungs burning with unshed tears. I didn't even get to the Scrub before Kyler's hand was on my shoulder.

"Wait," he said. "True."

I stopped for a second, my hands on my knees. "What?" I snapped.

"Don't worry about Old Man Parker. He's all bark and no bite. He won't tell your grandma. He's just crabby, and he doesn't—"

"Maybe it was my fault."

"What?"

"Teacup."

"No, it wasn't. You can't think that, True."

I couldn't help it—my throat choked on a sob. I ran, leaving Kyler behind. I had to get home. I cried the whole way.

By the time I got to the backyard, I was exhausted. Wrung out. My chest hurt from crying.

Everything hurt. My stomach. My ribs. My insides. I didn't feel good.

I felt wrecked.

I sat on the tire swing and cried until I couldn't anymore.

And while I did, the sun lowered in the sky until it became that purple-gray moment of the day, right between light and dark, a pretty, shadowy sky.

I spotted Rosie walking all quiet-like into the backyard, closing the gate carefully, like she was afraid of getting caught robbing a bank.

I watched as she scanned the yard. She hadn't seen me.

She had her wellies on. She moved near the back shed and hung something up on the back wall. It was her riding helmet!

So.

Compass Rose wasn't exactly following the rules either, was she?

When she started toward the back door, I called out, "I see you." She jumped about a foot in the air.

"True."

I got up from the tire swing. "So I guess only grown-up sisters get to break the rules, not stupid little sisters."

"Caleb Saint needed help today at the stables. And I missed the horses."

"The same Caleb Saint who you made that bracelet for last fall?"

Rosie didn't answer, but I didn't need her to.

"I can tell Dad at any time. Or Grandma."

"Or we could be on the same team." She gave me a smile, but then her brow furrowed. "What's wrong? Were you crying?"

I ran the back of my hand across my eyes. "Why do you care?"

"True, I care. I—"

"And don't give me any of that garbage about being on the same team. We haven't been on the same team for a super long time. Ever since you decided that I was uncool, that the Sister-Skate-a-Thon was too nerdy, and that I—"

"That's not true!"

Georgie appeared on the back porch. "True! You get that chicken coop cleaned yet? It's almost dinner, Gram says. And don't forget to fill Mom's hummingbird feeders."

"Fine! I'll be done in a minute."

I stalked off toward the gross chicken coop. I had let Teacup die—cleaning the chicken coop for all eternity was what I deserved. No, I deserved worse.

"True—" Rose called.

For once it felt good to be the one doing the ignoring.

Chapter 8

The next morning, I woke up to the sound of somebody or something banging against the floor of our bedroom. I felt the vibrations through the mattress. I flopped around for a second, confused. My eyes felt puffy from crying last night. Plus, the chicken coop had been an extra disgusting mess. I'd had to scrub. A lot.

I'd gone to bed early, too worn out from everything to even change into my pajamas.

Teacup. Her soft, paper-thin eyelids. Her still-curled-up ears.

Georgie had drawn a picture of her for me last night. I'd tacked it up on our bulletin board.

"Why do you think things have to die, True?" he'd asked me, his little face all pinched, looking like just the thought of such an idea hurt his brain . . . and his heart.

"That's a question too big for me," I'd answered.

The banging continued. I scrambled up, out of bed. What was going on? Then I remembered that sometimes Gram banged the ceiling with the broom handle to get our attention because she couldn't yell.

I was halfway down the stairs, in a panic, when I heard Rose's voice from the kitchen. I hurried in there, where she and Grandma Jo were talking, but Gram was using her white-board, not her magic-mic.

Rose turned to me. "What did you do?"

"I don't know. What did I do?" I thought of Teacup. Poor Teacup. Shame heated my face, my neck, my ears. I wanted to cry again.

Rose said, "Gram can't find her magic-mic this morning, and she can't find Georgie either."

"Georgie?" My heart clenched.

"I'll get my bike and ride around the neighborhood," Rose said. "Gram already checked the yard."

Gram's eyes pierced mine, telling me this was my fault.

I didn't know why, but I guessed it was. It probably was. I'd shown Georgie it was okay to break the rules.

I ran outside, falling down the mudroom steps, scraping my palms as I landed, but I didn't care. "George!"

Where had he gone?

He was just so little.

"Georgie!"

He didn't answer. How long had he been gone? How long had I been asleep? Why hadn't I woken up when he did? How had I ignored the Colonel and all his usual crowing?

George could be anywhere, doing anything.

Yesterday, I'd told him all he needed was the compass. I pictured him out in the Scrub with his stupid eyepatch and plastic sword, play-fighting, getting lost.

Oh figs. Oh figs. Oh figs.

"Okay," I said, and my heart thumped in my chest, my ribs tight. I ran toward the back gate, but just as I was pushing it open, George came barreling out of the Scrub. He had the big garden shovel in his hand and way too much dirt on his face. His cheeks were pink, his curls damp with sweat.

"I made you a map, True!" He was all happy-go-lucky, skipping over to me, but he must've seen the look on my face because he stopped up short.

"Where were you, George? Gram thinks you—Rosie's out looking—Ugh!"

"I was just out here. I wanted to cheer you up, True."

"Everyone thinks you're, like, dead or kidnapped or something! And where's Gram's magic-mic?"

"Well," George looked abashed for a second, and then it clicked.

"Oh no." He had always been kind of obsessed with the magic-mic, joking around with it, using it as his microphone when he played the karaoke game on the Xbox. Decorating it with stick-on rhinestones.

"It's just, I thought you'd have to find it, like I thought it was a good treasure. I got up really early and I had a plan and everything. I have the compass!"

I held my face in my hands. "You buried the magic-mic, George?"

His cheeks drained of color, and it was like he hadn't really realized what he was doing, why it might not be a good idea, until now. I watched the realization sink in.

"Oh boy. Is Gram mad?"

"Furious. But she's more mad about you going off by yourself. About me not watching you." I pulled out my phone and texted Rosie and Gram, so they would know I had him.

I'm going to find the magic-mic in the Scrub. Long story. Georgie is on his way into the house.

"I didn't think—"

"Right. You didn't think, George. Now get back home and let Rosie and Gram see you so they know you're alright. I'm going to follow the map and find the magic-mic. Give me a clue."

"Can't you just look at my map? Even though I made a mistake, can't you still use it?" He pulled his map from his back pocket, and he handed it to me, all defeated-like. It nearly broke my heart to look at it.

He had tried so hard.

But seriously, Gram's magic-mic?

I tried very hard to find a calm spot inside of me, one that wasn't annoyed. It was difficult. The best I could do was say, "It's a very good first try, George. Really good. Now the red X is near the, um . . . " I studied the map. "That's where we always see the dragonflies by the lily pads in the creek, right?"

George nodded, his bottom lip out like a sourpuss, his shoulders slumped. Clearly, none of this had gone the way he'd wanted. But, hey, join the club, kid.

"Get inside. They're waiting. Hurry," I told him. "And wash your hands."

"Okay."

I took off, not wanting to have to talk to Rosie or Gram again. I just wanted to get the magic-mic and let things get back to normal.

Or . . . whatever they were now.

⚘ ⚘ ⚘

I ran onto the trail in the Scrub, toward the creek bed. Had it really only been days ago when this path had been overgrown to the point we couldn't recognize every twist and turn?

When I got past the willow tree, I saw exactly where Georgie had been digging. I used my hands and uncovered the magic-mic pretty easily. It was smudged and covered with dirt, but I hoped and prayed it still worked. There were holes in the side of the thing, like a vent, and I worried there was dirt caught up in there. Could I clean it off without ruining it?

Jeez, George. Really?

I knelt next to the creek, and I wiped as much dirt as I could off the magic-mic, using the hem of my shirt and a little creek water.

I thought of Teacup, buried in her little cardboard box. I really should've made a grave marker.

Like a little pile of rocks or something.

Something caught in my throat then, a lump of bad feelings.

I looked up. I could see the trestle, and the barn was only just past it.

Gram wouldn't know if I hustled over to the barn for a quick minute. She would never know. I'd broken so many rules, what did it matter if I broke one more? I just wanted to find the grave again.

I took off running.

When I got to the barn, I saw Kyler's bike out front. I slipped inside and called his name, but I didn't hear anything.

I climbed up into the hayloft. Mustache and Eyepatch were asleep on the blanket, but Mr. Orange was awake and meowed hello. No Mama Cat around.

Movement from outside caught my eye, and I saw through the broken barn slats the spot where we had buried Teacup. I had chosen the spot well.

And right there, out by Teacup's little grave, was Kyler Grier. I hustled out to say hi.

"Hey," I said.

"Hey."

I pulled on my mask, just to be safe. He pulled his up around his mouth and nose. He hadn't put a stone on her grave, like I'd been thinking of doing, but he had put something else there instead. He had planted something.

"What is it?" I knelt down next to the little green plant.

"It's a sundrop. It'll bloom soon—bright yellow, like the sun."

"I was worrying about not being able to tell where Teacup was buried." My voice sounded funny, tight, like a stretched rubber band. "That's why I was coming here. I wanted to do something like this, but your idea is better. It's good. Real good."

Kyler nodded, his eyes watching me, all serious-like. "I'm sorry it happened."

"Me too." My stomach ached.

"What do you have?" He gestured toward Gram's magic-mic still in my hand.

"It's, um . . . the electronic device my grandmother uses as her voice box. I think it's technically called a throat-back, but we call it a magic-mic." I held it close to my throat, and Kyler nodded like he got it.

"Why do you have it?"

"Well, that's another story." I pulled the map Georgie had made for me from my pocket and handed it to him.

Kyler looked it over, staring real hard at Georgie's creation. "I like the way he drew the lily pads." He pointed at the magic-mic. "So that was the treasure?"

I nodded. "Can you believe it?"

"Wow, I bet he's in serious trouble."

"He sure is. So much trouble. I can't believe he'd be so stupid."

"He's little. He got excited." Kyler shrugged.

He studied the map again and pointed to a trail that George had named Rosie's Stretch, written in his little chicken-scratch handwriting. "I didn't know there was a trail here," Kyler said.

"There isn't. It's a trap street." I shrugged, rolled my eyes. "My mom told Georgie and me all about these tricks mapmakers used to use to make sure no one stole their copyrighted work, and that sometimes meant putting in fake stuff as a safeguard."

"Very cool. Like little top-secret clues."

"Yeah. Exactly."

"This right here, behind the tavern on Milkweed, is Old Man Parker's house." Kyler pointed it out on the map, between the Scrub and the western side of the barn.

"Oh, I didn't know that. I didn't know there was anything there." I made a mental note about how I'd have to amend my latest map of Spooner. It rankled me that Kyler might know more about this place than I did. I told myself it wasn't a contest, but it kind of felt like it was.

"Have you been there recently—to his house?" I asked.

"Yeah, I went by there today to dig up the sundrop. He told me I could—it was actually his idea—and . . ." A shadow passed over Kyler's face, and he pressed his lips into a hard line.

"What is it?" I rubbed my knuckles over my mouth. I could tell by the look on Kyler's face that he was going to tell me something I didn't want to know.

"I guess he went to the doctor this morning. His neighbor came outside and told me."

My stomach churned. "The virus?"

Kyler shrugged. "Don't know."

"Jeez." I didn't really know what to do with that information. Hearing about some kid I didn't even know in Trevor County who had the virus but who would probably be fine was one thing. This . . . I didn't know how to think about it.

Old Man Parker maybe had the virus. And I had been so mean to him yesterday.

Oh figs.

"I should go," I said. I suddenly wanted to be out of there. Away from Kyler, away from this new fact about Old Man Parker. And away from little Teacup buried in the muddy old ground.

I turned, but when I was a few steps away, I felt like I had to ask him, "Do you think that—No, forget it."

"What? What is it?"

"Do you think if I would've had the guts to take Teacup home with me before—if I would've just done that—do you think I could've saved her?" My voice broke, because that was a hard thing to wonder, and a harder thing to ask out loud to someone I thought would tell me the truth.

"I doubt it, True. I really do."

"It's not my fault?"

"It's not your fault." He held my eyes. I liked how nice his eyes were. Like they were trying to really know me, like they hadn't already made up their mind firm.

I nodded.

And then I ran fast. As fast as I could. Suddenly, all I wanted was Gram's robotic yelling. Georgie's apologizing tears. Rosie not caring about me at all.

I wanted to get home.

And not to think about Teacup. Or Old Man Parker. Did he have wires in him right now or a breathing machine like they showed on the TV news?

I tried hard not to think about how Georgie said Dad was coughing in the basement the other night after his shift at the hospital. I tried hard, but I still pictured it. I pushed myself harder, ran faster. I couldn't outrun that thought.

Chapter 9

Mom,

I think that the rules are sometimes stupid. That time when I got in trouble at school for wearing my tank top? Maybe I shouldn't have made such a big deal about it, but guess what? Now girls can wear tank tops like boys can wear muscle shirts. So there.

It's like, you follow the rules, you try to make a good decision, and you still get a bad, bad feeling in your heart because maybe it's wrong? Are there decisions that don't have a right answer?

And why should I follow any rules when the world has pretty much decided that the regular rules don't work anymore? No, you can't go to school. No, you can't see your friends. No Mom either.

No normal stuff.

Everything's chaos, so why should I do anything I'm supposed to?

Blimey. I'm sorry you can't come home. I know it's

not really your fault. I just hate it. I hate it so much. I miss you. Come home. I'm trying to keep Georgie happy. But it's hard.

It's hard to be me sometimes.

Love you,

True

I had the mouse hovering over the *send* button, about to send this email to my mother, but I didn't press it, because it made me feel sort of . . . naked and weird.

Just then, Rosie came in and sat on the bed next to me. She handed me her art tablet. Her good one with the expensive paper. "Here."

"What?"

"Just look." She sighed and flipped her hair over her shoulder.

I opened to the first page, and I saw a sketch of me with my head bent over a map. My eyebrows were all drawn thick and serious, like I was really concentrating. I loved the way Rosie had drawn my hair, like it was alive on its own, electric and in motion. It was always trying to get out of its ponytail, after all, even if it wasn't as curly and beautiful as Rosie's.

Next, there was a picture of Georgie laughing, his mouth wide open, his one chipped front tooth drawn perfectly. Next, a picture of me on my roller skates with Tamsin. I flipped through Rosie's drawings one by one. More and more pictures of us. Gram, asleep in her comfy chair. A close-up of

Dad's hospital badge. Georgie with the squirrel he and Dad trapped in the gutter last summer.

"I think I've been keeping to myself too much," Rosie said, her voice quiet. "Ignoring you."

I looked up at her. I expected to see the normal look from Rosie, the frown, the annoyed eyes, but, no, her eyes were . . . I couldn't tell. Sad, maybe?

She cleared her throat. "Thank you for not telling Dad about me going to the barn."

"I want to be a team."

Rosie sighed. My stomach twisted because I was so scared she wouldn't agree. But then she blinked real hard and nodded. "Me too, True."

She looked so young, like a version of me when I'm looking in the mirror.

Two sides of the same coin. That's what Mom used to say about Rosie and me. *Too alike to get along,* she'd mutter when we were fighting.

I realized something then, looking at Rosie's sketchbook. Maybe Rosie was trying to make sense of things with pencil and paper, trying to wrangle things in her heart, trying to keep some kind of control when growing up started to get to be too much.

Maybe sketching for her was just like me with my maps.

Suddenly, I wanted to help her. She was my sister.

"I know you have a lot going on," I said. "You have school,

and it's high school, not just fifth grade. You have your AP drawing class, and you do so much for Gram and—"

"That's all true. But I've been not such a great sister. I don't know . . . It's like I'm just waiting for this to all be over. I feel like I worry all the time now. I try to . . . I don't know."

"I know. I see everyone worrying, you biting your nails all the time. I know it's real—all these scary things."

Rosie reached out and took my hand. "I came in here because I just wanted to say that I don't want you to feel like you're alone . . . ever. Okay, True?"

I swallowed hard. Because that was exactly how I felt. Alone. Like I was the one responsible for holding it all together. Looking after Georgie. Worrying about Dad. Trying to help Gram and Kyler and Teacup. I didn't think I could say anything without blubbering like a baby, so I just whispered, "Thanks, Rosie—I mean, Rose—" My voice folded into silence.

Rosie watched me for a couple seconds, and then she said, "There was a girl at the stables, back when I used to be able to ride all the time. She was one of those girls with the unscuffed boots, the shiny new riding helmet. Her hair always perfectly braided. Wait, you know her—she's the girl who made fun of me, calling me a hillbilly when I had to get stitches on my forehead after that run-in with the Colonel."

"Oh, I remember. Lola? Lottie?"

"Lyla. Yeah. Anyway, she told all the other girls that any name that ended in an 'e' sound was a baby name, and she,

like, looked right at me when she said it." Rosie let out a huff
of breath. "I don't know why I cared."

"She's really mean," I nodded.

"Yeah. The point is, you can call me Rosie. It's okay."

"Okay." I felt Rosie squeeze my hand, and suddenly, I felt
like I wanted to offer her something too. "Tamsin likes boys
more than she likes books lately, even the boys that I think
are kind of dumb."

Rosie nodded like she got it, like she understood. Maybe
she did?

"Caleb Saint used to date Lyla. Maybe that's why I cared
what she said about my name."

"She seems stupid."

Rosie laughed.

I took a breath, then said, "You know, I was really sad the
Sister-Skate-a-Thon got canceled and you didn't seem to care.
You seemed relieved."

Rosie's cheeks flushed. She looked away for a second. "I
was, a little. It was the costumes. Millie and Jules teased me
about them last year . . . ah, forget it. I'm sorry, True. When
all this is over, when we get back to normal, I'll be . . . better.
We'll do anything, *everything* together."

I wanted to tell her that I loved her just the way she was,
that I just wanted her near me. With me.

Us together.

Us against the world. Us against all this craziness. Sisters
again.

But I couldn't really shape the words to explain it, so I just nodded.

Rosie tugged on my ponytail, gave me a smile, and got up and left the room with her drawing pad under her arm.

I sat still.

Something under my ribs felt tight and uncomfortable. Pinching in a weird way. Sometimes I felt like there was too much going on inside of me, like it was bubbling up and out and over, and usually it was my temper, but today, right now, it was more like my worries, how things felt out of control, and also, just *how much* I felt.

So many feelings.

Big, strong, overwhelming feelings. Feelings that filled me up until I thought I might pop!

Mom told me that when things got that way inside me, I needed to *do something.*

Like sixteen cartwheels in a row or run around the whole block or sing a song at the top of my lungs. I decided instead to draw.

I pulled out a big piece of butcher paper, but this time it wasn't going to be a map at all.

I started by sketching Mom, her corkscrew curls. But, no, that just made me sad. I ripped up the paper, crumpled it up. I cut myself another piece of paper.

I sat there for a long time, and I thought about little Teacup. I thought about the virus and the quarantine and

Mom stuck in Canada. I thought about the hospital and Dad, and I thought about Old Man Parker.

Maybe Teacup would've died anyway. No matter what I would've done.

Maybe my heart would've been broken no matter what.

Maybe Mom could've come home sooner, and she'd be here now, but maybe somehow something bad would've happened. Maybe luck kept her in Manitoba, kept her safe.

In the center of the page, I drew an empty circle. I kind of sketched around it on purpose. A blank blob, waiting for me to decipher what went there, fill it in later. But I knew there were so many in-roads and different trails and paths to get to this center location. I started on those right away. I knew those.

I used icons and words, text and pictures, lots of color coding and, of course, calligraphy on a glorious, beautiful compass rose, complete with a hidden cat symbol. I swiped Mom's colored pencils for the finished product.

I worked on it for hours, with Georgie hovering over my shoulder, still sniffling over his punishment because of the magic-mic. No graham crackers for two whole days.

Jeez. What an inhumane treatment, I had told him. *Cruel and unusual punishment.*

This new artwork I was making, this map of sorts, was exciting to me. But although I knew a lot of the parts, I didn't know exactly what I was making. It was like I was on a special kind of treasure hunt, discovering it while I was making it.

George asked me, "What is that, True?"

I answered him honestly. "I'm not sure . . . yet."

George nodded. When it came to the creative process, George didn't judge.

The next few days were boring.

We had e-learning. We didn't leave our yard. I had to wrestle George's eyepatch away from the Colonel because he somehow wanted it for his own. I weeded Gram's vegetable garden. Georgie and I had one million sword fights. I worked some on my new project—adding details here and there, telling George a thousand times I had no use for the skull-and-crossbones glitter he found on eBay.

Georgie and I helped Rosie frame her final assignment for her life-drawing class. It was a picture of Grandma Jo laughing, her head thrown back, her eyes sparkling with humor, her mouth turned up at the corners. It was a beautiful picture that made Gram's eyes tear up when Rosie showed it to her.

Tamsin texted me a million times because Miles McAlvoy kept riding his bike past her house.

Dad kept staying in the basement. I listened for the cough, but I didn't hear it.

And, of course, worrying about Dad made me worry about Old Man Parker. So much so that I tracked down Kyler's cell phone number through Cassidy Hauer, a girl from my gym class, who also lived in the apartment buildings.

I texted Kyler, but he didn't answer.

So finally, I called him.

"Hello?"

"Is this Kyler?"

"Yeah."

"Why do you sound like that?"

"Like what?"

My gut twisted. "I don't know. Scratchy." Was he sick? It dawned on me in that second that we had both been near Old Man Parker. Right before he got sick. How had I never put that together until now?

Had I brought the germs home?

"I'm not sick," he answered as if he had read my mind. "My mom is though. I'm quarantined."

Kyler's Mom was sick? "Is it . . . you know?"

"Yes."

Something icy and cold crept over the nape of my neck. I stammered for something to say. "I, um . . . I just wondered, um . . . no, never mind."

"Okay." Kyler sounded so tired.

"Is she in the hospital? Are you by yourself?" This all suddenly seemed so real. All my worries felt like they were stuck in my throat.

"Mrs. Hurn from down the hall checks up on me, leaves me food. Takes my temp."

"The library lady?"

"Yeah. She's really nice."

"You feel fine?"

"I feel fine."

"'Cause we did both see Old Man Parker, too, right before."

"We did. But we were outside. We had masks on."

"How is he doing? Do you know?" Did Kyler even have the energy to care about Old Man Parker when his own mom was in the hospital?

"I heard he's got pneumonia from it. He's in the hospital too. Worse than my mom."

Old Man Parker. He might have been a mean old bird, but I didn't want to think of him stuck in a hospital bed, unable to breathe. It was too much to picture. Instead, I told Kyler, "I'm sorry about your mom. How bad is she?"

"Thanks, True. She told me yesterday that she's feeling fine, just tired. She still has a fever, though, so they're keeping her there."

"You must be feeling so lonely."

"Mrs. Hurn brought me some books." There was something in his voice that I didn't like, a tell-tale tremor. I knew he was trying to sound brave.

I did that too. A lot. I recognized it.

"Text me if you need anything, Kyler. Okay?"

"Okay."

It was silent over the phone for a really long time. So long that I thought maybe he wasn't there anymore. I was just about to say his name when he said, "Maybe I could call too. Not just text."

"Sure. Yeah, call me. Whenever you want."

"I get scared, especially at night when it's dark and my brain keeps going."

"Call me whenever you want. I'm a talker, you know that. And Georgie could talk your ear off all night long, if you're desperate. He'll give you a pirate name, plan your whole next seafaring voyage. You'll be dying to hang up that phone."

He chuckled softly. I was hoping for more than that.

"Kyler, don't you have a grandma? Or someone who can come and stay with you?"

"I don't want her to come here. It's dangerous, you know."

"But, Kyler—"

"True, don't worry about me. Okay?"

"Okay." I rubbed my knuckles over my lip. I was lying to Kyler, of course. I would worry about him.

"Mrs. Hurn will be back soon. And you can't go telling anyone else I'm alone here, because that means trouble for me."

"What kind of trouble?"

"Bad trouble—like, you know, for my mom leaving me un-supervised."

"Okay." This felt dangerous. My heart thumped hard against my ribs.

"Did you read the book—the first Dragonmyth?"

"Not yet."

"You should read it. There's this one part in it with dragons. It's so good. The main girl, Arianna, she stands up to the head dragon—and she doesn't even have her spells yet—but she defeats him with just . . . I don't want to spoil it. You need to read it." He paused. "Arianna reminds me of you."

"Me?"

"Yeah, she's so brave. Real courageous and undaunted. Just read it, and you'll see what I mean."

"Okay, Kyler. I will."

"Thanks for calling."

My hands shook as I ended the call.

Suddenly, Old Man Parker was not the worst worry I had. I had so many of them now. And they were all wound up together in a big tangled knot of problems that had slid down my throat into the bottom of my stomach, like a rock falling into a pit.

No, Old Man Parker wasn't my only worry at all.

Not by a long shot.

Chapter 10

»»> ————> 🏠 <———— «««

After e-learning the next day, George was out of graham-cracker jail, so we sat at the kitchen table eating them. To me, they tasted like dust.

My phone buzzed. It was Kyler. He'd texted me another kitten gif. This one was going to war with a ball of yarn. I knew he wanted it to make me smile.

I'd told Kyler he better text me at least once every hour so I knew he was okay. So far, he'd been doing it. He'd called me and George last night too. George had read him part of *Pete the Cat and the Treasure Map,* and Kyler hadn't even seemed annoyed when Georgie had to stop and sound out words.

I was still worried about Kyler being all by himself, though. And all my other knotted-up worries. It's like I had backed my-self into a corner with no way out.

"True, what's going on?" Grandma Jo asked.

I guess I had been too quiet, staring at my phone, because Gram was on to me suddenly. She came over and pressed a hand to my forehead. I scooted away. I didn't want to give her any of my germs.

"No fever," Gram said. "But you look pale."

I looked up at Gram. I didn't know what to say. Or what to do. Things had gotten so big so quickly.

I felt like I was about to pop again.

Part of me wanted to ask Gram about what to do for Kyler.

But if I did ask Gram, would I have to confess to all the other stuff? Going to the barn? Seeing Kyler? Seeing Old Man Parker? The germs? The kittens—all of it?

Putting poor Georgie in danger, when he had asthma. Gram too.

My stomach churned when I thought about the virus being so close to Georgie or Gram. Why had I thought I knew better?

Suddenly, the graham crackers felt like a brick in my stomach. "I'm gonna be sick," I said, and I ran to the bathroom. I got there, just in time. I vomited in the toilet. I felt exhausted. So very tired.

"Honey, you okay?" Grandma Jo asked, running her hand over my hair, smoothing my ponytail.

"I am. Just got an upset stomach." And heavy worries.

"You want to talk?"

I shook my head.

"You want me to sit next to you while you try to take a nap?"

I shook my head again. But I did go up to my room and lay on my bed.

I decided I'd wait for Dad to get home. I'd stay up late and wait for him, and I'd ask him if he knew Kyler's mom and if he had heard anything about her, or about Old Man Parker. I'd tell him I'd been around him out at the old barn. I'd confess.

Dad would know what to do.

He was a nurse. He was inside these worries all the time. He lived there and worked in them.

Grandma Jo was just Grandma Jo, and I didn't know how to make myself say the words I needed to say to her. She scared me a little, if I was telling the truth. And, also, she was still mad about the magic-mic.

I really would've rather talked to Mom, but Dad would do. He would have to do.

He'd be disappointed in me. He'd stay real silent for a long time before he answered me; he always chewed over his words for a long time before he said them.

I didn't want to think about how he'd feel about me and my carelessness.

But I couldn't handle this on my own anymore.

When eight o'clock rolled around, George and I were playing Yahtzee in front of the TV, Gram was snoring in the recliner, and Rose came down the stairs with her phone in her hand.

"Dad's not coming home," she said. Rosie's face looked pale.

"He's not?" I squawked.

Gram startled awake. "What did you say?"

"She said Dad isn't coming home. Why?"

"What did he say?" Gram asked, eyeing Rose.

"He said he's under observation. I guess he had a temperature on the out-evaluation after his shift. He says he feels fine, but they gave him a test, and he has to stay quarantined until the results come back."

Oh figs. Oh figs. Oh figs.

"But he says he feels fine?" Gram asked.

Georgie started to cry. "I want to call Mom. Can I call Mom?"

Gram and Rosie exchanged looks, and I saw Gram melt a little for George. "Come on, baby," she said. Gram took his hand, and they went into the kitchen. "Of course we can call her. I'm sure she already knows all about Dad, but she'll want to talk to us. Let's call her."

Rosie and I stood staring at each other.

"I'm scared," I said, rubbing my knuckles across my lips.

"Me too."

She came and wrapped her arms around me. "We're in this together, True."

I didn't cry.

Neither did she.

I think, maybe, sometimes fear gets too bad, too strong, even for tears.

Chapter 11

That night, I curled up in my bed, staring at my phone as intently as Rosie did, all my fears and worries in a knot. Kyler was supposed to text me every hour until 11:00 p.m. I hadn't heard from him since 9:00.

I'd texted him at 9:03: *Any news on your mom or Old Man Parker?*

Then again at 9:30.

At 10.

Again at 11.

Nothing.

When I got out of bed in the morning—before the Colonel even squawked for the sun—the first thing I did was check my phone. Kyler had answered me around midnight.

Mom's okay. Old Man Parker's okay. Another guy from the stables has it though.

My stomach dipped. I worried my knuckles over my lip for a few seconds.

Cherry Hill Stables was the only place with horses around here. Probably for a lot of miles. That was where Rosie volunteered, at least before the lockdown. That must be where Old Man Parker kept his horses.

Had Rosie also been exposed to Old Man Parker's germs when she'd sneaked out to the stables? Or maybe from this other guy from the stables who now had it?

Things were getting worse and worse.

I dialed Kyler's number.

It rang and rang. Nobody answered.

My stomach did a somersault. "Oh figs," I said under my breath. But it was early. Maybe he was still sleeping.

George rolled over in his bed and let out a little fart.

"Go back to sleep," I barked at him. He didn't stir.

I called Kyler again, but it just rang and rang. On the third try, he answered, but I was sure I had the wrong number. His voice was a creaking croak.

"Is this Kyler?"

"Yeah."

"Why do you sound like that?"

"I'm . . . not feeling well."

My gut twisted. "How bad? How sick?"

"I'm okay, True. Calm down."

"Is it . . . you know?"

"Maybe."

"This started last night?"

He coughed then, so hard and so dry that the sound scared me. "Did Mrs. Hurn come over yet this morning?"

"No, but she texted me. She had to go to work early. But she'll be here after lunch."

"But did you tell her you're not feeling well?"

"I didn't want to worry her."

He coughed again, and my stomach lurched. "Do you have a fever?"

He didn't answer.

"Kyler!"

"Yes, I do."

"Does your mom know you're sick?"

It was silent for a really long time. So long that I thought maybe he wasn't there. I was about to say his name when he answered, "True, seriously I'll be fine. It's probably just a cold. I can wait for Mrs. Hurn. I don't want to go to the hospital. I don't want to worry my mom. She'll—"

"You're not thinking straight, Kyler."

"Don't worry about me."

"I can worry about you if I want to!"

"True, I have to go. I'm tired. I just want to sleep, and I'll probably feel way better when I wake up."

He coughed again, and I heard the beep of him hanging up the phone.

"Kyler?"

He didn't answer.

My hands shook as I ended the call.

I stood at the foot of my bed. Paralyzed.

What should I do?

What can I do?

I thought about helpless little Teacup. I couldn't wait for Mrs. Hurn to check on Kyler. I was not about to let myself repeat the same mistake again.

I had to do *something*.

It was way too early to wake up Rosie, but I didn't have a choice. I felt wild with worry, like I might blow up like a bomb if I didn't *do something* right now. If I didn't act.

I rubbed my knuckles over my lips as I stood over Rosie sleeping in her bed. How much was I going to tell her?

All of it.

"Hey," I said, and I shook her shoulder.

Of course, the Colonel seized that moment to crow at the day breaking. But that ear-piercing squawk was a welcome sound because Rosie stirred.

She sat up and rubbed at her eyes. "True?"

I sat on the edge of her bed. "Rosie, I need you to come with me. I'll explain on the way. I just . . . I think we have to hurry. And I did some things. Made some reckless kind of choices, and I'm worried about my friend."

Rosie leveled a look at me. "True, what are you talking about? Wait, you have to tell me first and—"

"Do you know Old Man Parker?"

"From the stables?"

I nodded. "He has the virus. And so does someone else from the stables."

Rosie's eyes went wide. She got out of bed and grabbed her phone, quickly scanning the screen. "I have, like, a zillion texts."

"Okay, but we have to go now. I'll explain on the way."

She started pulling on her jeans and a T-shirt, and I took that as a good sign, but then she said, "We have to ask Gram. I need to tell her what's going on."

"No, we can't. She won't want us to go. No way, no how. We just have to do this. Please, Rosie. I'll explain it all, confess it all." I thought about Kyler in his apartment all by himself. I thought about Mrs. Hurn getting there too late. I thought about Teacup and I thought about the sundrop planted behind the slanted barn, and I had a sudden urge to cry. I choked back on a sob.

Rosie looked at me hard for a long moment. "Okay, we'll slip out the back. Go write a note for George. Tell him to wait for us here and not to leave the house. Tell him we'll bring him back a surprise if he behaves."

"Good idea."

I felt my breathing settle down a little bit. If I couldn't have Mom, or even Dad, at least I had Rosie.

We were a team.

We had to check on Kyler. We would stay six feet away from him. We would be safe with masks. We would keep him away from Gram. I would not endanger Georgie.

I would just check and make sure Kyler was okay. I had to see for myself. I had to get his mother's number or Mrs. Hurn's. Something. I had to act. Not just leave him there by himself.

The Scrub was cheerful and beautiful so early in the morning, full of buzzing insects and chirping birds. We hustled through the Scrub in no time, and I explained it all to Rosie. Every last thing. I confessed to all the dangers and chances I'd taken, all the promises I'd broken.

"And you know Gram would want to come with us to check on Kyler. She'd be over here, trying to cook him up some chicken and dumplings, and we can't have that."

"No, we can't," Rosie agreed. "Gram just got over voice-box cancer. We have to be careful. I was so careless to go to the stables. I don't know what I was thinking."

"I wish Mom was here."

"Me too."

When we got to Kyler's apartment building, Rosie and I were both huffing and puffing from the trek. I wiped the sweat from my forehead on the back of my hand. I noticed my fingers were shaking when I pressed the button for Kyler's apartment. His last name was next to the buzzer, printed out on a pretty green tape.

At first, there was no answer.

"I can't believe he's all by himself," Rosie said. "Seriously."

"He's not answering."

I tried again.

Nothing.

"Maybe I should try Mrs. Hurn," I said, pointing at her buzzer.

Rosie's phone gave a little ding, telling her she'd gotten a text. She looked down at it, and then she looked right back up at me, her eyes wide. Scared.

"It's Caleb Saint. He's the other one at the stable who has the virus."

"Oh, Rosie. He'll be okay."

Her phone rang. She answered it, and I stubbornly rang Kyler's buzzer for what seemed like twenty minutes straight. Eventually, the door going up the stairs buzzed even though there wasn't a voice or anything from the intercom. I realized just in time that the buzz was the door unlocking. I grabbed the handle and pulled it open. I turned to Rosie over my shoulder. She was still on the phone.

"Just stay here. I'll be right back." I didn't want her to get too close to Kyler, if she could help it.

Rosie nodded.

"I'll call you if I need you." I bounded up the steps. I had my mask on and a pair of surgical gloves from Dad's stash. I knocked on 2H. It was easy to find, the last one on the right. No one answered.

I kept knocking. "Kyler!" I whisper-yelled.

When he finally answered the door, my stomach fell, just plummeted right out of my body. At least that's what it felt like. He was not standing. Instead, he was on his hands and knees. I realized immediately he didn't even have enough energy to stand up.

I knelt next to him, put my arm around him, and helped him crawl back to the couch. I fumbled with my arms around his waist, his weight leaning on me. He was burning up, his skin felt like a furnace or a lit match. I pulled him toward the couch, and we managed somehow to get there, but then he shook me away.

"I'm okay. I'm okay. I just sat down on the floor because I thought I was going to pass out. I'm okay."

I stepped away from him. He crawled up onto the couch by himself, then he heaved himself into a sitting position. The whole apartment smelled like the minty, medicine-y stuff Gram rubbed on George's chest when he got a bad cold.

I couldn't quit staring at Kyler. I was in disbelief. He looked scary. Dark shadows under his eyes. This strong, big kid had seemed invincible just days ago. Heck, he had been talking to me just yesterday like nothing was going on.

"I'm fine. Mrs. Hurn will . . . be here later, and . . . Mrs. Delrose—she works with . . . my mom."

When he talked, it was like he couldn't get enough air in his lungs to say more than a few words at a time. He moved his limbs like they weighed a thousand pounds each. And I could hear each one of his breaths, a crackling kind of inhale and exhale. He coughed, and it sounded hard and dry, like a bark.

It scared me. No, it *terrified* me so bad that my knees knocked.

I wanted to leave.

I wanted to leave so bad.

I wanted to forget I ever came here. I wanted to believe Mrs. Hurn and Mrs. Delrose could handle this, that they had everything under control. I wanted to turn around right now, sprint home, and go straight to the shower to make sure none of these germs got to Gram or Georgie.

But I couldn't move.

I stood there, doing nothing, when Kyler's cat—a big, fluffy gray thing—jumped into his lap and meowed. He seemed worried about Kyler too. Kyler couldn't even lift a hand to pet him. He just sat there.

There were so many water bottles on the end table next to the couch, a bottle of Advil, and a zillion used tissues. The TV played a home renovation show, and I knew it was only because Kyler was too weak to reach for the remote control, clear on the other end table. A vaporizer was plugged in beside the TV, and cool mist shot into the air. But I had a feeling Kyler needed more than a vaporizer and Vicks VapoRub.

He needed a nurse. A hospital. He needed a grown-up.

Kyler had closed his eyes. Could he already be asleep?

I walked closer to him. "Hey," I whispered.

He opened his eyes. "I'm just so tired, True. You can go. You *should* go—really. Not be around my germs."

Kyler's cat meowed again, then jumped from Kyler's lap to the floor; he rubbed his head on my legs. I felt like the cat was telling me to do something. Fix Kyler!

I saw the skin around Kyler's mouth looked blue-ish. Like Rosie had said about Georgie, when he hadn't gotten enough oxygen during an asthma attack when he was little.

Kyler was turning blue right in front of me.

A shiver, cold and terrifying, struck down my spine.

I thought of Teacup. Of how I hadn't done anything to save her. How I'd been too scared. I couldn't just leave Kyler here.

I didn't care if he had twenty-seven nurse neighbors who were supposed to check on him tomorrow morning. He needed help now. Right now. Right this very second.

I sprang into action.

"Can you walk?" I asked.

Kyler took a breath, and it squeaked going in. His eyes got wide, and he shook his head.

"Even if you lean on me the whole way?"

"No, True."

"I think you have to try."

"I don't want to . . . give you . . . my germs."

I grabbed a paper mask from his end table and tossed it to him. "I have my mask on. And you know what? I'm not giving you the choice. We're going. Now."

I dipped down, and I pulled his heavy arm around my

neck and shoulder. "On the count of three, we stand up, okay?"

We said it together: "One . . . two . . . three."

He stood, and a whole heap of his weight—most of it, maybe all of it—leaned onto me. I didn't care. I didn't think about it. I had one goal. The map in my mind had one location. My house.

I'd get Kyler home to my house, and I'd tell Gram to call Dad. He would know what to do.

He would know what to do for sure.

Dad. I wished I had my big, quiet, strong Dad right now.

I had to get Kyler home. Right now. Rosie was outside; she could help.

But we weren't even to the door of his apartment when Kyler mumbled something.

"We can do it. We have to," I told him.

He didn't answer me, and I felt him go limp next to me. His knees buckled, and he was too much for me to hold up. I tried, but I couldn't keep him upright. I ended up going down with him, clumsily trying to keep him from hitting his head.

We tumbled down, me screeching "No!" while his limbs tangled into mine, and I lost my footing. I was able to land somehow, some way, with his head in my lap. He was safe.

"Oh figs, oh figs, oh figs."

I looked around. We sat in the little foyer of his apartment, and I was so nervous I could barely think. Kyler had passed out right on top of me!

I pulled his mask down and checked his breathing. It was still coming. Crackling away. In and out.

"Are you okay?" I said to him. "Kyler?" I tried to shake him a little.

Nothing.

I managed somehow to move myself enough so I could pull my phone out of my pocket without jarring Kyler too much. Why hadn't I done this to begin with?

I didn't know.

I dialed the phone, my fingers too shaky to hit the correct buttons. I had to retry three times before I got it right.

"911, what is your emergency?"

"My friend passed out. I think he has the virus. His mom isn't home right now."

"Can you give me the address?"

"I don't know it." I started to cry. Here I was, the map-maker, and I couldn't even give the one detail, the one location, that was needed.

"Just stay on the phone. We'll track it."

"I'm just a kid," I said. "My sister's here too. But I'm just a kid."

A drop of blood dripped onto the screen of my phone.

I realized I had hit my head when we landed, the corner of the little table in their foyer leaving a sharp gash on my temple. I hadn't even noticed.

I felt a sob building up in my chest and more tears streamed down my face.

"Please stay calm. We'll be there soon. Help is on the way," the voice on my phone said.

"I'm just a kid."

"You're doing great. Is your friend breathing?"

"Yes, ma'am, but his lungs are working too hard."

His nostrils flared. His eyelids fluttered.

"Wait! He's waking up. He woke up. He's looking at me!"

"You're in the Heath Apartments. Which number, dear?"

"Um . . . 2H."

"We will arrive in less than three minutes."

"True?" Kyler said. He closed his eyes, then swallowed like the motion hurt him.

"I called an ambulance. You're going to be okay."

I wasn't sure that was true, but it looked like he believed me.

Chapter 12

True,

Your father has kept me up-to-date on all that has happened, and if I know you, then you're probably lonely in your quarantine in the basement. It's boring, I bet.

That old toilet makes a lot of scary noises in the middle of the night, doesn't it?

But you are so brave. You are so very brave. You have a courageous heart and a wonderful, giving, thoughtful spirit. But please remember that you are a child. You are not required to have all the answers, nor do you have them. There are some problems that need to be handled by adults.

Because sometimes, True North, there are decisions that have to be made in life that will weigh heavily on a heart for years to come, no matter which way you go with them. Kids shouldn't have to do that when they are still so young.

Such decisions are for grown-ups.

Because these decisions have a difficult compass to read, the needle won't always point north so
clearly. Do you understand what I am talking about?

I'd like to talk more about this with you—and your
sister, your dad. And Georgie too.

George video chatted me today. I'm so very sorry
about Teacup.

Dad says Kyler and his mother are doing just fine.
Mr. Parker is okay, too, so far.

Kyler is probably only going to get better so
quickly because of you, you know that? You are a
hero. I am chuffed. But also, I'm sad about your silence, luv.

Love,

Mom

🌲 🌲 🌲

It took me two days to read *Dragonmyth: A Nomad's Tale.*
Rosie felt sorry for me being stuck in the basement and went
to the library to get me the second book. She left it at the top
of the stairs for me, along with my breakfast.

I'd already written Kyler the longest email about the first
book. I'd been so flattered that he'd thought of me when
Arianna slays the dragon, because she didn't even have her
magic yet. But she had something extra-powerful—her courage

and the truth. It was a magnificent story, with a bunch of amazing side stories—elves and trolls, a magic mirror that saw into your soul, and a talking ferret—and I loved it.

And Arianna reminded me of myself too, actually. She was brave and smart and cunning. But she wasn't perfect at all. She was learning along the way.

Kyler had already written me back, which I figured meant he was already feeling much, much better. Able to write emails. Able to badger me into telling him what I thought might happen to the Goblin Prince in book two.

My family worried that I was too lonely in quarantine. Grandma Jo said over and over that she wanted to take care of me and make me my favorite green bean casserole and that I shouldn't have to quarantine all by myself after what happened, but I felt like it was a punishment I needed to do. A caution I had to take. I owed it to George and Gram.

And to Rosie for helping me. For being on my team.

She was wearing a mask all the time in our house just to be safe, but she hadn't been up close and personal with Kyler or with anyone at the stables, so I was by myself.

But that was okay. I owed it to my family because I had been . . . careless. Too careless. Gram had been right all along. I didn't think the rules applied to me.

Now, I saw how serious it all was. But also, I didn't like how grown-ups tried to act like kids couldn't think their way through a difficult decision.

That seemed unfair.

I needed to talk this over with Mom.

I scrolled to her number on my phone. I hovered my finger over the *send* button on my phone, and I realized in that split second what Mom had been trying to tell me.

That I should've talked to her from the beginning. At the start of all this—the barn, Teacup—if I would've just talked to her . . .

Finally, I hit the *send* button and immediately connected with her.

"True!" she answered, and my heart flipped at the sight of her face, the high, round apple of her cheeks, and the way her two front teeth overlapped just a little bit. It all was so familiar to me. So very dear to my heart, as Grandma Jo would say.

"Hi," I said, the back of my throat already stinging with tears.

"Oh, my darling girl." Mom's eyes were wet with tears.

My eyes started to shine too.

"Mom." My voice cracked.

"Oh, honey, let me look at you."

I let her look her fill until, after a long moment, she asked. "What's that?"

"What's what?"

"The project, the big paper behind you."

I turned to see that Mom was asking about my work in progress that I'd pinned up on the bulletin board. I focused the phone on it, so Mom could see it more clearly. "This is

what I've been working on, Mom. It's some kind of map—but
. . . an *impossible* map."

"Oh, True."

"Look, there in the middle, there's just a blank spot. I
don't know the location. I don't know where all these things
are heading to, you know? Do you see what I mean?"

I adjusted the phone to zoom in on the paper so Mom
could really see what I had drawn, all the details, the big missing center of it.

It suddenly seemed important that she help me figure out
where it was that I was trying to go, the map, the location, the
place.

"Mom?" I said, keeping the phone turned to the map on
the wall. It seemed easier to say the things I had to say when
her eyes weren't on me. "I'm sorry I put people in danger,
especially Gram and George. I'm sorry for all this."

"Let me look at you," she ordered.

I brought the phone back up to my face, feeling a bit shy.
Ashamed, really.

"I'm sorry you were left so alone in all this," Mom said.

I nodded at Mom, trying to fight back the tears.

"Can you explain to me what you've drawn on your
project?" Mom asked.

"Well, it's like . . . I have all the in-roads, all the paths coming to the middle. There's a winding path to the slanted blue
barn and the spinning pig weather vane. Here's the dragon

compass buried beneath the willow. And a trail of books circling around the whole paper."

"And what was that at the bottom—the thing that looks like a tornado coming out of nowhere? Oh, I see. They are in each corner, moving in, like gusts of wind."

"Those are my worries," I said. It felt like there were so many of them.

"Hmm. Very interesting. And you just don't know what goes in the center, huh?"

"Yeah, like I said—it's like a map, but not a regular map. An impossible map. I want to take all these things that are important to me, and I want to find a way out of this trouble right now. A new place. A safe one. I don't know. It sounds goofy, Mom, but—"

"It doesn't sound goofy at all, luv. Listen, here's a question for you. Why do we make maps?"

"To show someone how to get somewhere."

"Well, now, that, I think, is a close answer, but not a complete answer. Think again."

I paused, studying the lines and arrows on my map.

"We draw maps so we can show someone all about a place. So they can get to know a location or a subject," I finally said.

"Yes, you are exactly right, luv. There's your answer, True North."

"Where? What's the answer?"

"This project that you're working on is not a map in the literal sense. It's deeper than that."

"Hmm," I said. I thought maybe I was starting to see what Mom was talking about.

I looked at the butcher block paper then, all of the details I had added. The Percy Jackson symbols flying a path toward the center of the page. The Scrub itself, and its winding footpath. A sketch of Rosie on a horse, traveling due north. Georgie with his pirate sword, running toward the chicken coop.

Kyler's eyes above a mask. Roller skates. The magic-mic with its rhinestones.

A teacup turned into a compass rose.

And of course, there was a trail leading to Manitoba, Canada, and a road to the hospital where Dad was quarantined.

This was a map of me and everything I cared about, both the things that made me happy and the things I was worried about.

But it wasn't a true map because all the paths and roads were tangled up, like a maze, an impossible labyrinth.

"Mom," I said, starting to understand.

"I think what you've done, True, is that you've drawn your heart on the paper. *You* are in the center of your map. True North Vincent. And all your ins and outs, every single complicated heartstring, is telling people how to get to know you, to appreciate you."

I cried then.

I cried so hard I had to put my phone down and just let it come. "I'm sorry, Mom. I tried to do my best. I tried. I was selfish, and I just—"

"You're fine, True. You're just fine. This is a terrible time."

She knew I was talking about more than the impossible map, that I was talking about all the mistakes I'd made, all the secrets and all the risks.

"True, I want you to understand something: there are problems that have no good answer. No good solution. You are a very smart girl, but you have to trust that some things are too big for you right now. Because sometimes, no matter what decision is chosen, there can be serious, sad, awful re-percussions that can't just be on a kid's heart, okay? So you need to have a trusted grown-up on your side. You have to tell us before things get too out of control, too big for you."

"I didn't think . . . I just . . . "

"You did just fine, honey."

"I should've talked to you."

"Yes, but things are going to be okay. Dad just has a reg-ular old cold. Gram's fine. Georgie's fine. Rosie, too. And I'm fine. So don't fret, luv."

"This is all so scary."

"It is."

"If this is what being a grown-up is like, having all these bad choices, and no good answers to horrible problems, well, then, no thanks. I think I'll stay a kid."

"Good choice," Mom said. "But growing up isn't just about making hard decisions. It's more. And I think you know that."

Mom smiled and touched her fingers to the camera in the phone, a tender gesture. "You gave Georgie your compass."

"He loves it."

"Can I see your impossible map again?"

"Sure." I held it up to the phone.

"Ah," she said, "that's what I thought."

"What is it?"

"The thing is, True, you need to add one other thing to the center, right next to your name, or whatever you choose to add that symbolizes you."

"What should I add?" I looked at the paper again.

"Something to symbolize me—alongside you. Because you're never alone, okay? No matter where I am. You will always have your family standing next to you, helping you and loving you."

I smiled. Mom was right. She always was. About everything.

"Maybe I should draw a . . ."

"I got it!" Mom said, chuckling. "How about an éclair, the world's most useful—and my favorite—measuring device?"

"*Pishposh*," I told her. Because I was laughing too. Then I had it, the perfect idea. "I'll draw in a hummingbird for you, yeah?"

"I'd love that, True."

Mom always joked that I was her "True North" because it

was, after all, my name, but the thing was, Mom was mine too. She was always there for me. Always in my heart.

Mom. Her voice in my head and in my heart—it was a map all in itself.

Not just helping me get from one point to another, not just giving me directions through life, mapping me through decisions, but helping me know myself.

True North Vincent.

Because, after all, even if I wasn't exactly perfect, I was pretty great.

Acknowledgments

A heartfelt thank you to the entire team at Shadow Mountain—Chris Schoebinger, Heidi Gordon, Breanna Anderl, Troy Butcher, Callie Hansen, Haley Haskins, and Ilise Levine. Special thanks to my editor, Lisa Mangum, for loving True and her story with such understanding and exuberance. Thank you to Richard Erickson for the extraordinary cover, Rachel Murff for the fantastic map of Spooner and True's beloved Scrub, and Kevin Keele for the terrific illustrations.

Also, thank you to Caryn Wiseman, my agent extraordinaire and tireless champion of children's literature. Thank you for all you do.

And, of course, a special thank you to Zoe, Maia, and Jack. My inspirations, my true norths.

Discussion Questions

1. Why do you think True and Georgie love the Scrub and the slanted barn so much? What are some places that you love? Why?

2. True has a difficult time making her mind up about Kyler at first. True's mom told her that she should make up her own mind about people. Do you agree? What do you think True eventually decides about Kyler? How do you think she comes to this decision?

3. Why do you think Teacup means so much to True? Do you think True should feel responsible for what happened to Teacup? Why or why not?

4. True seems to get annoyed at her friend Tamsin sometimes, as well as by what Tamsin thinks is important. Why do you think that is? Do you have any friends who you disagree with? Do you think this is okay?

5. When True experiences some big, overwhelming feelings because of all the things going on inside of her, she says it feels like she's about to "pop." Mom said that when True

feels like that, she needs to do something, "like sixteen cartwheels in a row or run around the block singing at the top of her lungs." Or draw. Have you ever felt that way? What do you like to do when you feel this way?

6. Why do you think True likes to draw maps so much? What are her top three reasons for loving maps? Do you have anything you love like True loves maps?

7. True's relationship with Rosie changes throughout the story? Why do you think that happens? Why does being Rosie's sister make True sad sometimes? Do you think this is normal between sisters? Why or why not?

8. Describe True's relationship with her parents. Do you think True handled it well when her mother was unable to come back home? What do you think she should've done differently?

9. Describe Grandma Jo. At one point, True admits she's a little scared of her. Why do you think that is? What does True mean? Do you think she still loves her grandma?

10. Do you think True waited too long to tell someone about Kyler feeling sick? Why or why not? What grown-up would you go to if you had an overwhelming problem?

11. If you made an impossible map of your own, what would you include?